SETTRIGHT
ROAD

SETTRIGHT ROAD

STORIES

JON BOILARD

DZANC
BOOKS

DZANC BOOKS

5220 Dexter Ann Arbor Rd.
Ann Arbor, MI 48103
www.dzancbooks.org

SETTRIGHT ROAD. Copyright © 2017, text by Jon Boilard. All rights reserved, except for brief quotations in critical articles or reviews. No part of this book may be reproduced in any manner without prior written permission from the publisher: Dzanc Books, 5220 Dexter Ann Arbor Rd., Ann Arbor, MI 48103.

Library of Congress Cataloging-in-Publication Data

Names: Boilard, Jon, author.
Title: Settright road : stories / by Jon Boilard.
Description: Ann Arbor, MI : Dzanc Books, 2017.
Identifiers: LCCN 2016017550 | ISBN 9781941088623
Subjects: LCSH: City and town life--Massachusetts--Fiction.
Classification: LCC PS3602.O47 A6 2017 | DDC 813/.6--dc23
LC record available at https://lccn.loc.gov/2016017550

First US edition: January 2017
Interior design by Michelle Dotter

Printed in the United States of America

10   9   8   7   6   5   4   3   2   1

CONTENTS

For Dad, Susie, and Uncle Meatball

Fear not them which kill the body, but are not able to kill the soul.

Matthew 10:28

JUST THE THING

I sniff paint thinner in Bobby the Killer's garage. I'm supposed to be mowing the lawn, and he'll be pissed. I'm only living with him because he's banging my Aunt Haylie and she has custody. They met when he fixed the tranny on her car—a two-door, four-cylinder rice burner with a hatchback. She couldn't get it out of first gear. He's got a little shop in a barn behind the garage where I'm sitting on a stack of studded snow tires and looking out the busted window.

The sky is strange, a crack of blue and clouds and pink. The glass-faced thermostat reads ninety-nine degrees and the humidity is always a bitch this time of year. I can hear him pounding on an alternator with a rubber mallet. It's an old red-rusted Jeep. It's just me and Bobby right now because Aunt Haylie is slinging beers over to the VFW. She used to dance at the Castaway Lounge but the Greek told her she was too fat for that anymore. She cried from bed for three days straight. Then she met Bobby. He'd just moved down from Turners Falls.

He's different, she said to me. It's gone to be different. You'll see.

Maybe I don't want it to be different.

But this might be just the thing.

Those are only words, I said. You used the exact same ones last time.

That conversation was two months ago and now I guess we're all settled in.

I look at the lawn mower and it's not moving. I look at the grass outside and it's not getting any shorter. We don't have much of a yard really. Patches of green and dirt and stones and little tufts of blond that remind me of cunt hair. Tools hang from the wall on nails bent this way and that. A bag of fertilizer. Some weed choker. A red gas can. A few old buckets of paint.

I always know when Bobby the Killer is nearby because he smokes skinny drugstore cigars called Swisher Sweets and he stinks of them. Right now he's standing in the doorway with his thumbs in his pockets. The knuckles are missing skin, and his arms are missing pigment.

What the fuck, he says, shaking his head.

I tell him I'm taking a break.

He makes a fist with his right hand like in slow motion, holding it down by his hip. Then he opens it and shakes his fingers loose like from a spider web nobody else can see. A blue vein throbs on the side of his cow-skull head. A cigar sticks out from the straight line that is his mouth. He chews the end of it, looks at me for a minute. I smile back at him but not nice.

Bobby turns away and grabs an orange box from under the workbench. It's heavy plastic with metal latches, smudged with axel grease. His name is printed on top in black magic marker. He pops it open, grabs an adjustable wrench, stares at it. Thinking about what to say to me. What to do about me. I know for a fact that he wants to bury that wrench in my face.

Bobby the Killer wants to do me harm.

But that will land him in the doghouse so he retreats.

That fucking lawn won't mow itself, he spits on his way out.

I try to picture the lawn mowing itself and I laugh out loud. Loud enough so he can hear me, that silly redneck fuck. Then I go inside to take a nap because it's too goddamn hot for chores anyhow and plus my brain is beginning to shut down from the stuff I inhaled.

When I wake up, it's dark and quiet, which means Aunt Haylie is working another double shift and Bobby the Killer is losing at cards and getting shitfaced drunk at the Polish Club with all the other old guys in town. The air is a bit more bearable when the sun goes down. There's a Mason jar in the refrigerator full of pickled eggs floating in a pissy brine. Bobby's mom makes them for him and his sister, who lives in town, too. I take one, and then another, and don't stop until the whole jar is gone.

A few minutes later Brenda Pasnaki is knocking at my door. She's wearing strawberry lip gloss and a wife beater and black short shorts. Pearls of sweat on her shoulders and chest like a necklace. I know her from school, which I don't always go to for all the usual reasons.

She bats her eyes at me—something she got from MTV.

Hey, I say. You here for your lesson.

Yeah, she says.

I open the door wide so she can come in and then I tell her to follow me to my room.

I'm teaching her how to suck a dick.

She smiles and blushes, snaps her bubblegum with her tongue. We go into my closet and study up on some of Bobby the Killer's porn. Afterward I tell her she's getting much better.

Loads of improvement, I say.

She's very pleased. Among other things, Brenda is also a perfectionist.

I pull up my pants and we smoke a joint that tastes skunky and watch cartoons. Tom and Jerry crack me up, always into some shit. Brenda craves French fries and a chocolate frappe and so I take cash from the drawer in the kitchen where Aunt Haylie hides her tips. I get my BMX bike from the garage and she sits on the handlebars and we ride down the middle of Pleasant Street against a warm breeze that carries with it green-eyed horseflies and the chemical smell of the tannery. Last year after drinking two bottles of Boone's Farm and a pint of Jack Daniel's, I hotwired an El Camino with Jimmy Peters and drove it into the man-made pond. Jimmy can't swim and so of course we got caught. Chief Waz made us pick up trash at the drive-in movie theater every Saturday for a month. Milk Duds, Junior Mints, Mike and Ike, popcorn containers.

Chip Flanagan is half-sitting on the black handrail in front of the pharmacy. Puffing on a Kool. He graduated a few years ago. He works at the package store now and will sell me booze out the back door. He drives a sweet GTO and keeps a wooden baseball bat in the trunk in case there's any trouble, and there usually is. He's parked the car under the dim light across the street and it looks like it's just been washed. Blue and shiny and dripping water. Chrome bumpers like funhouse mirrors. Chip doesn't notice us until my rear brakes squeak and he looks up, turning slightly so Brenda can see his new tattoo. He got it at Johnny Palomino's Ink Shoppe off Route 2A in Bernardston. It's a red rose wrapped around a knife blade on his right bicep.

Oh, hell no. Look what the cat done drugged in, he says, flexing his pipes a bit.

Brenda gets down off the bike and I lean it against the brick wall. She fixes her shorts from going up her ass and tries to ignore Chip, but I know he gives her the creeps.

He offers me his cigarette and I pinch it between my fingers and take the last couple drags. We pose hard like that and look across the way at his GTO.

She's a real beauty, I say.

Oh yah hey, she's a fucking beaut, he says, looking at Brenda instead. Chip somehow thinks of himself as a ladies man.

His left arm suddenly jerks skyward like he's a puppet on strings. Eventually his hand flaps back down to his side like a scattershot bird. He has a mild form of Tourette syndrome that manifests itself in occasional and uncontrollable spasms.

It's one of my favorite things about him.

Brenda rolls her eyes and goes inside the pharmacy and Chip whistles through gray, clenched teeth and adjusts his balls and calls me a lucky somebitch.

I don't see it that way.

Then he wants to buy a dime bag of dope so we make a plan to hook up later. Brenda is already in the booth and by the time I join her she's already ordered for both of us. Pat Roy with her blue beehive hairdo is running the counter and she shakes her head when she sees me—her daughter is my age and I popped her cherry last Fourth of July at the Dwire Lot barbecue. Pat drops potato wedges into boiling oil. The frappe machine motor whines. Then she puts the big bowl in front of us. Two metal containers overflowing chocolate and two glasses with straws.

I squirt ketchup on my fries one by one.

We feel better after we eat.

Brenda looks at me and says she wants to go home and fuck.

Much later I open my eyes and Bobby the Killer is naked. Brenda is crying, and Aunt Haylie has a bonehandle pistola. The living room is mostly dark but for the blue light of the television. I'm sitting on the couch in my tightie-whities and Aunt Haylie is looking at me but pointing the gun at Bobby, who in turn is trying to hide behind Brenda. Brenda's shorts are around her ankles, but she is covering her bare tits. I smell gasoline and the pink goop that Bobby uses to clean his hands. And I smell just-got-after pussy, which is another clue as to what is going on here.

It's surprising to me, but not unbelievable.

The only sound is Brenda sobbing and a high-pitched hum from the off-air station on the television. There's an empty rubber hanging off the end of Bobby's limp dick. He pisses himself in fear. The rubber fills up and falls off—splat—and I'm the only one who seems to notice.

Well, Aunt Haylie says to me.

It seems she has asked me a question and is waiting for an answer.

What you got to say for yourself, she says.

I don't know what to say to her. I'm still trying to piece it together.

Whoring your little slut out to Bobby, she says.

I laugh out loud.

Look at her, she says. How could he resist.

I look at Brenda and Aunt Haylie is right. She's a beautiful girl and maybe I have created some kind of monster. Brenda looks at me and tells me she's sorry but I don't really care about that. Not at all I don't.

Aunt Haylie's gun hand is shaking. Bobby is shaking too and he puts his hands over his cock as though that will help.

The front door flies open and Chip strolls in with his Louisville Slugger. Riding around like he will and I guess he witnessed my predicament through the window facing the street. He stands next to me, twitching like somebody is shocking him with electricity, and leans on his bat. He checks out Brenda, gives Bobby a look, nods at me and half smiles toward Aunt Haylie.

He was a regular of hers at the Castaway Lounge back in her stripping days.

Then at once his body settles back into itself, and sounding cool, unflappable, and maybe oblivious, he says to my aunt, What's up. He angles himself so she can see his tattoo, but Aunt Haylie ignores him.

A dog starts barking in some backyard and that gets a whole gang of them going like a strange and far-flung church choir.

Well, I finally say. He ain't so different, now is he. You always want different but nothing ever is.

Aunt Haylie lowers the bonehandle pistola to her hip, which is Bobby the Killer's cue to bolt for the door that Chip left ajar. She watches him disappear into the night, starts to cry and sits down on the floor. I take the gun from her gently and put it in my waistband. We hear the pickup engine start, tires squeal. I wonder where he'll go now, driving off without any clothes.

Brenda gets dressed. Her wife beater is all bunched up on the floor near the coffee table and Chip fetches it for her, holds it to his nose before he hands it over. She's regaining her composure now, standing straight. She snaps her gum. Her running makeup is clown-like.

You want a ride, Chip asks her as she tugs her shirt on.

All right, she says, looking down at her feet instead of any-where else.

He winks at me.

They leave together and close the door.

His fat Eagles chirp too.

Now it's just me and Aunt Haylie, like it always has been since my moms split for Florida when I was a kid. We stay put for a good long while, her crying and me rolling a fatty. Then I put my arm around her and she rests her head on my shoulder. Then we smoke together. Her cheeks are red and puffy. Her T-shirt smells like fabric softener and peanut shells and the underarm roll-on that balls up where she hasn't shaved. There are crickets in the bushes alongside the house and Aunt Haylie says we've got to pack up and get out before he comes back with the cops. I remove the bonehandle pistola from my shorts, tilt my head, and aim the gun at the television screen where from this angle ghostly figures are moving—old images that got stuck in there somehow, bad memories. I tell her about an apartment above the Bloody Brook Bar in the center of town. I saw a flyer on the wall in Rogers and Brooks. It has new carpet and curtains, and a Sears microwave.

She nods her head up and down until her chin rests on the hard part of her chest.

That wouldn't be too bad, she says.

Her voice sounds funny, muffled. She inhales and holds the stuff deep in her lungs as long as she can. Then she closes her eyes and exhales. I can smell her breath like stale milk.

That might be just the thing, she says.

Opens her eyes and blinks them to adjust. I can feel her looking at me.

Then she sighs my name and smiles at the ceiling. And I squeeze the trigger and there's a flash of white and the gun kicks, the meaty part of my arm jams back into my shoulder socket and all those bad memories trapped inside Bobby's box explode into a million little pieces.

SIX STONES DOWN
THE MOUNTAIN

The Malibu fishtails then stops and the man asks if you need a ride.
His radio is playing music from Northampton and you get in. It's a
hot one, he says, and then he tells you his air conditioning is on the
blink. It just needs a shot of Freon, but he hasn't gotten around to
it. His mouth is so thin and straight and looks like it was made with
a knife. He keeps his left hand on the wheel, steering with his wrist,
and he takes the back of your head with his right, holding your hair
so tight your eyes water. Don't move a muscle boy and won't nobody
get hurt, he says, putting your face in his lap. Then he turns onto
Sawmill Plain Road just past the Sitterly lot.

Mumbling the words to maybe a church song you don't recognize:

> Six stones down the mountain
> Six stones down the mountain
> Lonely as it is up there
> Looking for a god that cares

You hear a flat-bed from Austin Brothers, but what you see are
the mostly red wires spitting copper venom, all that remains of the
Malibu's dashboard. His long-sleeve shirt smells like motor oil and
armpits. He waits until a couple cars pass and then he cranks the

wheel and under the hood a loose belt giggles sinfully at the apparently familiar predicament. He sets you on your side, undoes your trousers, pushes them down below your hips. He tugs your underpants down too and stretches the waistband trying to get his greedy fingers exactly where he wants them. Oh Jesus. You close your eyes against the sunlight and sense the afternoon:

> *Hobo zooms his crop duster over Tapscott's fields. You hear the thresher out in Fat Johnny's hay and that old FarmAll tractor is coughing up a lung. You hear the rolling words of some Puerto Ricans hired out of Holyoke as they gather around the water pump for their break. You smell the manure pile at the edge of Thurow's property and hear Peter Junior shaping it with a backhoe. You smell the diesel fuel in Paul Soloski's pond from when his nephew got drunk and tried to set it on fire. You smell the exhaust fumes of RVs with New York plates as they back into position at the White Birch Campground. Jimmy LaPinta's Willys is skipping a cylinder in idle as he pitchforks heads of cabbage into the back. They thump and bump against the makeshift rails he's constructed out of particleboard and plywood scraps. He'll try to get a load to Oxford Pickle before supper. Then Mark Williams is having trouble with the Jamaicans he buses in from Hartford for the harvest so his corn is still high on Meadow Road and it swallows you.*

The long stalks rustle until you emerge spent from the guts of that seasonal green beast. You skirt the landfill, where Chet Pellovicz is known to nurse a nip of Jack Daniel's in the woodshed, sucking on orange slices, waiting to collect the next random toll. Fat black horseflies and blood-drunk mosquitoes buzz like power lines and Big Billy Borden's far-off hammer secures the frame of Doc Compton's new house out past the drag strip. The red vinyl seats of the Malibu scorch the exposed skin from where the stranger has maneuvered your clothes, and they moan when he moves you against them. Your face chafes against the lap of his starched khaki pants.

The river is privy to bigger secrets that you will never tell. It shushes you and shoves trout down toward Stillwater Bridge, where fly fishermen in hip boots cast their lines patiently smoking Swisher Sweets, standing in shadows. The river is running high because they've let the dam out at Old Squaw Reservoir and it hisses and spits and slithers on its stark white belly across Franklin County, from Bardwell's Ferry to Bloody Brook to Cheapside.

Then the transitory lullaby of Wingo's milking machines humming. When you get onto Lee Road the melting sherbet sun drips through the driver-side window and you almost feel it on your tongue. There is something else, too, that tastes like a ten-penny nail. Another electronic click in his steering column signifies the new stop sign just propped up at Route 116 and Lee Road, and he guns the engine, no longer careful. Then the Malibu slows down some.

Sit up now, boy, and fix yourself, he says.

You do as you're told with Sawmill Plain Road coming up on the right.

Which house is it, he says. Where you stay.

You show him the house your father rents from Ned Karkut.

That's good, he says. Now I know where to find you.

He licks his fingers like after a Sunday potluck at St. Matthew's Church and he smooths out his eyebrows. He smiles sluggishly, drunk on something other than liquor, and half-sings:

> *Six stones down the mountain*
> *Six stones down the mountain*
> *Lonely as it is up there*
> *Looking for a god that cares*

The man pats you on the knee, reaches over and opens your door.

Now don't tell nobody, boy, he says. Or I'll come back and pop one a them nuts.

But he didn't have to say those words, you already knew you could never tell.

The Malibu U-turns and throws ghosts from its tailpipe. Your mother's forsythia bush sobs soft yellow blobs that scatter, the weathercock wrestles the wind. Your father's pickup is backed up to the long barn, which means you're late filling Addison's grain and water buckets. You hurry and check the salt licks in the north pasture. Beyond Ostroski's patchwork fields the sun slips behind the sawtooth scalp of Sunsick Mountain and the sky is spilled pink lemonade.

Your father turns toward you and in the near dusk his face takes on a blue-metal hue like it's forged of the same stuff they make shotguns from. Stray cats so skinny they're just brown bags of sticks hide in the glooms high up on the rafters, and they watch you with vampire eyes.

DARK DAYS

At dawn the sun is staining pulled-taffy clouds various shades of purple and orange and Maureen sits by the aluminum deer stand like Nick told her to. There's a skinny white dog at her side. Maureen does not see Nick at first because of the angle of his approach but when the dog barks and wags its ass she stands and smiles. Nick walks over to her and she puts his face in her hands. They kiss hard, her tongue still in his mouth when she starts to cry.

The dog sits. Maureen pulls herself together.

I brought this for you, she says.

Nick looks at the dog.

To keep you company, she says. On the run.

Oh, right.

It's from Malek's, she says.

Malek is the dogcatcher. He shoots them after ten days and the crazies even sooner. Nick puts his hand down to the dog and she sniffs at his fingers and palms.

My grandma rescued it, Maureen says.

What I'm gone to do with a fucking dog.

Give it a name for one thing.

Is it one of those crazy fuckers, Nick says.

Why would that trouble you.

I don't need no more crazy.

Running like you done wrong, she says. That's what's crazy.

Right.

Ought not pay for your father's sins.

That's what you say.

Just 'cause he got Junctioned again.

And this time that fag judge will stick me somewhere too.

You don't know that, she says. You're not like them others.

What others.

Your father and uncle and them.

Shit, girl, he says. I'm exactly fucking like that.

Maureen turns her head violently as though she's been slapped.

Folks say Eddy rescued you, she says after she collects herself.

Nick laughs.

That's one way to look at it, he says.

You got a place.

We had a place.

She looks surprised and then disappointed.

I thought your uncle had a girl or something, she says. With a place.

That didn't work out. He ain't really the girlfriend type.

Maureen and Nick climb the wood ladder up to the elevated metal shack and the dog barks as they ascend. The door hangs on a single hinge and Nick pulls it aside with one hand and knocks down cobwebs with the other. She follows him inside. They sit on a dirty old mattress and she makes a face and sneezes. She has healed up nicely from the attack—he tells her again the details of how he settled things with those boys that had done her like that. It's clear that he gets more from the telling than she does from being told. Then they lie back and touch each other until she feels better, but he can tell her parts are still tender.

The dog is barking like crazy down below.

How long we gone to do this, she says.

Oh, I'm almost done.

She laughs, says, I don't mean this right now.

Nick knows what she means. He doesn't say anything for a little while and she goes back to work on him. Then he's finished and she kisses him fast on his mouth until he pulls away. He closes his eyes. It's a rare moment of comfort that he'd like to stretch out for a while.

So, she says.

Fuck, he says. So what.

Can't just hide in the woods like some hermit.

All right then.

Not with that wildfire.

Right.

Hot embers every-fucking-where.

I know, he says. I seen them.

My daddy says it's like Dark Days.

Shit, he says. That was a long time ago.

The hills are burning.

It's a bad world, he says. I've told you that.

That's what I'm saying.

I mean, crossing the street can be dangerous.

Whatever, she says. Got half a mind to bring Westy next time.

Nick throws her a look and she knows she has crossed a line. He pushes her off his lap and stands and fixes his pants and belt.

That's a fucked-up thing to say, he says. Take it back.

I take it back, she says. I truly do.

She reaches up and gets hold of Nick's hips. I said I didn't mean it, she says. Please, Nick.

You can't even play like that, he says. Or we're through.

Don't ever say we're through. And she cries. It seems to Nick like she is always crying about one thing or another. She stands up, too, and he gets her to calm down a little bit, but she is shaking now like some kid. She snaps her pink bra and tugs her T-shirt down over it.

Jesus fucking Christ, he thinks. Maybe my uncle is right about females. Come on now, Nick says. Stop it.

I'm sorry.

Don't be sorry, he says. You just can't do like you said.

I know.

This here is some shit, he says. Some real shit.

I know it.

All right then.

But the damage is already done. Nick sees trust as a length of firewood and when Maureen threatened to bring the local police, well, it was like she chopped off a piece of it with an axe. She doesn't say anything else and they hold each other for a while, but he has to get back so that his uncle doesn't get suspicious. There is a cow behind an electric fence switching its coarse black tail at fat black flies. He watches the bovine over the top of Maureen's head until she speaks.

Well, she says. Maybe I can run with you.

Nick laughs, can picture how that would sit with his uncle. He rests his chin on her scalp and softly exhales at the flakes of dead skin in the dark roots of Maureen's dyed-blond hair where today she has parted it straight down the middle. Out the rectangular plastic window, in the near distance, is a cool-eyed timber wolf already with its thick winter pelage. Gray brown and stiff-legged and tall; the word regal comes to mind. It's looking back and forth between the cow and the barking dog with its ears erect and forward, and Nick runs his fingers along the scabs on Maureen's arm.

Uncle Eddy boils river water in a metal can that is balanced on some rocks over an open fire. He sits on his haunches and watches it start to boil. He pokes at the flames with a stick. There is a frying pan off to the side so he can cook up the half-dozen eggs they stole from Len Boulanger's henhouse by the apple orchard. He has not looked at Nick for a long time and he will sure as shit not look at Maureen, who is next to him, wrapped in an old wool blanket. Eddy pulls the sleeve of his flannel shirt down a little so it covers his hand, takes the metal can from over the fire, and rations out the boiling water into three chipped cups. He rests the metal can in the dirt where Nick had cleared it with some hemlock branches.

Come on now, Eddy says. Get you some. Spitting into a pile of saw-logs he indicates Maureen with a backhand wave.

I won't say much on the topic, he says. But I will say this.

Nick and Maureen look at him.

She shouldn't fucking be here, he says.

Maureen looks at Nick and Nick looks at the fire. He kicks dirt at the fire with the steel toe of his boot, and the dog barks.

For the record, Uncle Eddy adds. Not happy about the dog, either. But at least we could eat the mutt.

He doesn't look up when he says it. Then he puts his cup to his mouth and rises and blows a little and takes a sip and closes his eyes while standing still. Nick gets up, too, and walks over to get his and Maureen's drinks.

Maureen pulls her sleeves down and holds hers like that and she closes her eyes and the steam floats up into her face. Nick stands next to where she's sitting and puts his hand in her hair.

Uncle Eddy looks at her and then he looks at Nick. This ain't no life for a pretty little thing, he says. That's all I got to say on the matter. Then he turns to fixing the eggs. Well, that and also she might've been followed, he says. He looks straight at Nick when he says it. Which I warned you about.

He puts the pan over the pit, resting on the same two rocks he used before and after a minute he spits into it. When his saliva sizzles and snaps away he cracks the eggs two at a time into the pan and chucks the shells over his shoulder. He turns them with a stick and puts them over the flames until they thicken just enough and pop yellow and white. He lifts the pan out and puts it in the dirt to cool—the damn dog sniffing at his legs the whole time. Uncle Eddy, Nick, and Maureen sit together and rest atop a carpet of leaves under a blue-lavender sky. They eat with their fingers and the dog whines and yips at Maureen.

Then it's as though somebody turned out the lights.

Eddy looks up.

Fuck me, he says. We're deep in it now.

Nick follows his uncle's upward gaze and Maureen does the same.

With tiny dappled shadows on their faces, they can see that the sun is being blocked by black ashes, falling from heaven like the delicate feathers of a thousand scattershot birds.

STORM CHASER

I pressed plates at Cedar Junction for fifty cents an hour. It could've been worse and I didn't complain much. There were blacks and Puerto Ricans who hated me. I hated them, too. I threw hands enough to get some respect but not so much to cause me any real trouble. Dope smoking was forbidden although easy to do and that's what got me through. Plus my girl would visit my dreams now and then. I still call her that, even though I know it's not true any-more. Cassie couldn't wait for me and I don't blame her one single bit. She was a dancer when I met her and we'd hit it off right away. It was a place in South Hadley called An-thony's and I did a million deals there—mostly small-time stuff, which was my bread and butter. I wasn't greedy but I had a certain territory to protect. Sometimes things got rough and I usually came out all right. Cassie worried but you know how it is when you're on top of the world; nobody can tell you anything. Then somebody dropped dime on me and my cousin Mick swore it was Cassie but I refused to believe it. Upon my release, I drove by her trailer against my better judgment. There was a boy playing in the yard, he looked nothing like me and that hurt like hell. That's when it hit me what those years in the Junction could take from a bad man, had taken from this one.

The boys are on the beach blowing up GI Joes with firecrackers. They use seashells and bottle caps to hide the miniature bombs. I drink Jack Daniel's and watch from the porch. A hurricane is coming, and fishing boats and lobster traps are already washing up on the shore. Seagulls dart and nervously flick themselves at the rickety old wood-rigs named Shirley and Abigail. Then the thin German swimmer from next door cuts a razor-straight and smooth-stroked swath to No Name Island, past catamarans upended and dinghies and Timothy Donovan's latest Boston Whaler.

My father bangs on the upstairs window with his fat hand. He's telling me to call the boys, to get them into the house to safety. I ignore him. I always ignore him and have since I was a kid. I know they'll be all right. They're always all right. No matter what terrible shit we do to them. I finish the bottle and stand the dead soldier on the rail.

Then I burn about half a joint down to a nub.

My father is behind me now; I can feel his angry breath on my neck. With the folded-up sports section of the *Boston Globe* he fans the air around my head, making a real production out of it, letting me know that he doesn't approve of the marijuana as well as most of the other things I do. But I stopped seeking his approval a long time ago.

He coughs and spits.

That's some real fucking weather out there, he says.

My court-appointed therapist calls that keeping the lines of communication open. Too little, too late as far as I'm concerned. My father and I haven't had an actual conversation in a decade.

I'm going for a walk, I say.

He dry coughs into the inside of his elbow.

I descend the spiral metal stairs at the end of the porch and cross the yard to the cement wall that will soon fight the rising tide. Johnny Cash is coming hard from Paul Calupetro's condo and Paul salutes me with what I would guess to be his sixteenth highball as he and his wife of forty years dance like young honeymooners on their new deck that's about to be decimated by a cyclone named after a famous whore. There's a strange sense of urgency that comes over a coastal town when a big storm is brewing, as though everybody is trying to compress their pathetic lives into the span of a few hours.

Super Cop is making the rounds on foot, busting balls, trying to get people indoors. He's got a bullhorn and a long flashlight. He sees me and so I cross the street because a run-in with him is the last thing I need—that fucking guy has been arresting me for years.

The tough young dudes at the pier smoke long Kools from Cumberland Farms and flex sunny muscles for a polished blond girl from the Bath and Tennis who sips diet soda through a straw and giggles. She's beautifully oblivious to the danger that looms. Beneath them in the shadows a brackish and blackening tide slurps and slaps hungrily at the barnacled and tar-stained posts that strain against the weight of time. The high whine of an outboard motor and the sharp smell of gasoline cut across the cove and disappear blue past Cunt Cave and then around the point. The haunted house is leaning north and east there, one-dimensional, featureless against the low-hanging fog, a missing piece in a too-complicated jigsaw puzzle. Slow-tracing the horizon, a tanker slogs toward Beantown, hauling cars or sugarcane, a sooty plume dangling in its wake.

I round the corner at the old Amoco sign that swings noisily from a chain, past the commune and the Crab Pool. I catch my breath on a rocky edifice and Super Cop taps me on the shoulder, which startles me.

Hey, Storm Chaser, he says. What's it doing.

The nickname catches me off guard. I haven't been called that in a while.

Fuck me, I say. You shouldn't sneak up on people.

Super Cop laughs. His actual name is Brady Fillmore.

Brady and I came up together and were pretty tight until around junior high, when he started going pretty fast in one direction and I had already gone too far in the other. In seventh grade we'd skipped school, broken into my father's liquor cabinet, and spent the day drinking vodka with orange juice in front of the oversized, fake-wood-framed television. There was a show on that afternoon about a man who lived in his van and followed hurricanes up and down the East Coast—measuring wind speed and rainfall, keeping notes, taking pictures and videos for the sake of posterity. He referred to himself as an amateur storm chaser.

Even in our inebriated condition, we were intrigued. We watched the entire show.

That's what I'm going to call you from now on, Brady had said to me when it ended.

What's that.

Storm Chaser.

Fuck you say.

The way he positioned it was that instead of running away from storms, which is what most sensible people do, this guy on television would run toward them. It was all in the name of research, but it seemed he was innately drawn to trouble. Going against all human instincts. In my case, he noted, there seemed to be a similar need to thrust myself into the middle of shit.

Minus the scientific purpose and humanitarian motives, of course.

Earth to Sean, Super Cop says in an attempt to return me to the here and now.

I was just thinking on the good old days.

I suggest you find a safer place to do that, he says. This one is a real bitch. Then his walkie-talkie cackles as he gets called away to

break up a domestic dispute. It sounds like the address of Paul Calupetro's condo, and I picture his wife of forty years wielding a kitchen
knife. I imagine Paul throwing a metal chair through a window. Domestic discord at its finest.

Super Cop turns his back to me, talks into his shoulder.

I take the opportunity to slip away.

Seaweed specks the coastline in brown patches. Blood-purple jellyfish
roll over for one decisive sting, horse flies leave large red welts, and
sandpipers do their silly sand dance. Dark groove-number buoys
and fishnets define the dry dock where Joey Mongeon weighs the
day's catch, thick fingers fumbling, poking at the intricate switches of
the scale. The August breeze carries with it the flavors of the rowdy
clambake at the south end where the public is allowed: a smoking pit,
the crink-tinkling of cheap beer bottles breaking.

Then a daunting dusk rips the world asunder.

Perfect darkness drops in stages like a carpet bomb campaign,
bonfires appear and pop teenage delight. Eight-cylinder American
engines howl around Blount Park, white-wall tires screech in wicked
syncopation, stereos spill vintage Van Halen and Def Leppard and
Bon Jovi into Lexington Avenue, backdropped by an odd cacophony
of crickets. Somebody shakes a clacking can over his shoulder and
spray paints the words SUCK SHIT on the glass storefront of Collin's Bike Shop. Other drunks, older and more established in their
vices, stumble from Lion's Lair smelling of pizza and Jameson and
two-stroke motor oil.

My father bought the apartment here with money he made selling grinding wheels for Bendix, and now I'm staying with him as part
of the conditions of my parole. There is some wealth around town,
but it's mostly working class. The Magnolia Bath and Tennis Club is
off limits to people like me, although I know my way around a little

bar called the Fort. It's dark inside and just a handful of other regulars and of course Sally McNamara pouring drinks. The Red Sox are on the television. I order a whiskey and bitter. Sally is wearing tight faded jeans and a pink tube top. She's barefoot, as usual.

Her husband, the owner, is out front hanging sheets of half-inch plywood over the windows that face Raymond Street. With the storm getting closer, he's having a tough time staying on the ladder. His face is turning red and he's holding nails in his mouth, they're sticking out like rusty vampire fangs. I watch him struggle and not even for a second do I consider lending him a hand. He comes inside when he finishes his task. He's soaking wet; a real mess. Sally laughs at him. She hates his guts and I'm screwing her on the side so I laugh along with her but not because it's funny. It's more complicated than that. He removes his vintage Carl Yaz No. 8 T-shirt, throws it at her, and she ducks. It lands with a splat on the floor behind her and cowers like a dying thing.

She picks it up and rings it out in the stainless-steel sink.

You fucking prick, she says.

You ungrateful cow, he says.

Even their bickering lacks passion.

He slaps me on the back and tells Sally to give everybody one on the house, which is a rarity. She shakes her head but does as she's told, another rarity in itself.

Sally rings the bell, we all drink up.

Then she brings me a bowl of salted peanuts.

The man of my dreams that one, she says to me in a hushed tone.

I look at her husband's reflection in the long mirror behind the bar. He is short, fat, hairy and pale; not somebody who should be walking around in public minus a shirt, but he doesn't give a rat's ass. That's what I love about the guy.

Like I said, it's complicated.

His name is Bob or Bobby Mac to his friends. I guess he was some kind of all-star ballplayer back in the day, but you wouldn't know it to look at him now. And that gets me thinking about all of my former selves: the son with potential, mighty patriot, brother with a spine, the protector of innocent children.

How far the mighty have fallen, I think.

Sally wants to close up shop like every other business in town, but Bobby Mac tells her to relax. He wants to make a couple extra bucks off the storm. Get something out of it besides the opportunity to haul sandbags from the cellar. Eat, drink, and be merry, he says. For tomorrow we're all fucking dead.

He isn't supposed to drink. There are a stack of DWIs he has to consider, which maybe he does just before he streams the cheapest rotgut directly from the bottle into his throat. Then Collin from the bike shop emerges from the shitter and stands next to me and tells me that he's just seen my big sister, Lisa.

In the shitter, I say in mock amazement.

He guffaws and removes the coaster from the top of his glass of house wine that had been setting there the whole time. If I had noticed it, I would have sat somewhere else on the off chance that it was his.

She's a fucking cunt, he says. She almost ran me down.

Collin has a way with words. He's quite known for it. A real gift. He's spitting bits of chewed peanuts on me when he talks. I turn the other way to avoid the shrapnel, but he won't let it go.

What's her problem anyway, he says.

I can feel him staring at the back of my head, waiting.

He repeats himself, and the muscles in my neck begin to tighten. Collin lets out an impatient breath that smells like clam dip.

Besides being a cunt, I say, hoping against hope that that's the end of it.

But it never is with guys like Collin. That is one thing I know for sure. Some people just can't leave well enough alone. There's really only one way I know how to end this conversation.

Your family, he says as though those two words form a complete statement.

I wait a couple three heartbeats before turning back around to look at him. Please, I say in the nicest way possible. Just shut the fuck up.

A simple request because I'd rather not get any deeper into it with this clown. I'm trying to turn over a new leaf and all that. But he's really pushing my buttons.

I'm just saying, he says. That cunt has problems. And then he's off and running again, showering me with his peanut bits and harsh words. Jesus fucking Christ. I guess I should have seen this coming a long mile away. And I guess I actually did.

He is right, though. My sister does have problems. Lots of them. For example, the state is in the process of taking the boys away from her, and justifiably so. She blames me for it and claims that I turned them against her. They're young and don't know any better so they love her anyway. But none of this is any of Collin's business. He doesn't have a right to weigh in as far as I'm concerned, on my sister or the boys or any of it. It's a family matter. So I tune him out as best I can. But eventually I can't take it anymore.

I close my eyes. And I know again what it means to see red. Then that familiar sensation inside my brain—a rubber band stretched to its limit. I open my eyes. And there's no stopping me now, no turning back once I get to this point.

I reach up and take his windpipe between my thumb and bent index finger. An efficient and almost gentle human transaction. And I hold him there at arm's length. It's a subtle move I learned from a skinhead at Cedar Junction. Collin flails about trying to break free but I've got him trapped. He's quickly losing his wind. His drink goes flying everywhere, and it would probably be comical to watch if it weren't so fucking sad. Bobby Mac rushes over and tries to make me stop.

Jesus H. Christ, he says in my ear as he karate-chops my forearm.

I let him try for a while, but he can't break my grip, the funny little prick. I shove him aside with my other hand. Ex-athlete or no, he's not used to dealing with a man like me. He's got a certain strength that's developed on the playing field, but my power comes from a deeper well. A darker place. And there's just no match. So he gives up.

People are freaking out now and there's a lot of commotion around me, but I stay focused on efficiently disposing of the perceived threat of the moment; and that is my true gift, a skill honed in barrooms and back alleys and various state correctional institutions. I learned a long time ago that only during violence can I correct my mistakes in the very same instant that I make them. And that's the beauty of it, this brutish thing I do.

I watch up close as Collin's face turns different shades of blue.

Call the motherfucking cops, somebody says.

The war hero has gone mad, somebody else says.

Well, if I have, then it was a short trip.

After a while I release Collin and his legs give out and he falls down, his limbs collapsing in on themselves like a marionette puppet whose strings have been cut.

Bobby Mac helps him sit up on the floor.

Collin is covered in peanut shells and he massages his throat and his eyes fill up with tears. He tries his voice box but it will be a few minutes before it works again. Bobby Mac stands him up and guides him by his elbow to a stool far away from me.

Sally gives Collin a glass of tonic.

He sips some of it and coughs.

Sally looks at me and makes her way over. What the fuck, she says.

I take a long pull from my drink because I don't want to talk about it. Not with her, not with anybody.

Sean, she says, leaves my name hanging in the air.

Exactly how much shit I'm supposed to eat, I say.

She knows what I mean. She holds both my hands in hers until I take them away. Think about the boys, she says.

When am I not thinking about the boys, I almost say.

You'll end up back inside with moves like that, she says.

You say it like it's a bad thing.

Sally is a tough woman but even she starts to cry at that comment. Is that what you want then, she says.

You don't understand what it's like for me out here.

But is that really what you want, she says. Caged like an animal.

I don't fucking know what I want.

That's always been your problem.

Inside at least they tell me, I say. They tell me what I want.

I finish my drink and put the empty glass on the bar and go outside. Collin is calling after me; every name in the book. His courage is up again and he wants to put on a show for everybody now. But he's smart enough to stay inside. Good for him.

Be the victim, you fucking shitbag.

Go ahead and get the crowd behind you.

Semper Fidelis, motherfucker, he shouts at the top of his lungs.

I try to light the roach from earlier, but the wind and rain prove too much. Plus I'm shaking. My hands are shaking the way they always do after a good session.

The moon is a half-lidded eye, lazily surveying the hard little town that is slowly devouring me. I look up at my father's apartment across the street and the boys are in the window—perfect faces pressed against the glass fogged with their breath. I almost smile and wave from my hip but they appear to be sobbing and trying to tell me something urgent. Maybe Lisa has gained entry; she's a resourceful one and always has been. She has a key and my mother won't let my father change the locks even though there's a restraining order because Lisa has claimed on record that if she can't have her sons then nobody can. Or maybe the storm has the little one spooked, the bending trees reminding him of skeletons. Then the boys disappear from my view, like a dream. I want to go up there to put them at ease, toss their hair, sit with them in the big chair, tell them everything is going to be all right, but I'm no longer convinced that that's the truth. A stronger force is pulling me back into the bar to finish what I started.

At first I think it's the wind again, but what I hear is a police siren getting closer and closer.

THE MOHAWK TRAIL

The burning red of early swamp maples and a singular stand of white birches and a picket fence snaking along a hillside. My father parked the truck, and I breathed deep. The name of the place was Joey Mitch's Horizons. There was a band there that afternoon but I don't remember what they played. It was loud. Everybody was dancing and having a good time already. It was Saturday. I was on a stool at the bar that squeaked whenever I turned around to look at the drums and the people. There were three grown men with the hardscrabble beginnings of their winter beards playing pool. They looked up one by one and called my father Buddy.

My father knew the bartender too. Then they were drinking shots of Jim Beam. My father ordered a glass of Michelob. And then another. The bartender's name was Billy Fitzsimmons and they used to work the pits at Hinsdale together. My father told him about the 1967 Mustang convertible he picked up in Bernardston. He called it a cherry. He told him you could eat off the engine. He talked about the Windsor heads and the TRW pistons and the rebuilt V8 302. It runs like a top, he said. His hands were thick and nimble and dark-grooved with axle grease.

Autumn hills were blushing gold and copper and a pale purple, but the gray threat of winter was lurking in the form of a cold snap and I remember outside my bedroom that morning bare sugar maple branches had been scratching at my window, beckoning, trying to lure me away from my father's house. Then Fitz gave me marshmallow-topped hot chocolate because I could see my breath even indoors, even with the fireplace, a fresh log just tossed in and crackling. Paper-thin black flakes floated like broken promises when a pretty girl poked it with a black iron stick. I burned my tongue a bit. Fitz laughed, told me to go easy on the hot toddy. He said something else funny to my father and he looked at me and winked. I liked this man already. A hunter in a Double D's cap called his name at the other end of the bar and he went to serve him.

My father touched my arm and said, Just a little while more. He called me Sport. He stayed looking at me when I faced the long mirror behind the rows of bottles. There were pretzels in a salad bowl. Fitz came back and asked my father if I was the next Yastrzemski and my father told him that I was a chip off the old block. We played catch in the backyard sometimes before things got too bad. Pop flies were my favorite. My father threw the ball so high sometimes I waited forever to snag it. When he wasn't around I practiced on the dented roof of the barn. Then my father shook me. It's time to go now, he said. Come on now, boy.

In the glare of the dying day, that mist-filled dusk, my father's face was red and his nose was red and his eyes were red around dime-sized black buttons. His skin deep-pocked like some rotten old rind. He walked almost sidesaddle, like he was going to fall, and then he put his hand on my back, the whole weight of him bearing down.

We climbed into the old pickup. He stuck his head out and got sick on the door, then put the steering column shifter in neutral and hit the clutch and turned the key and a sputter and a rumble under the heavy hood soon became a hum.

Route 2 toward Charlemont was jammed from Perry's Pass to Whitcomb's Summit. We drove behind what my father called the leaf peepers. They came from the city to look at the fall colors through fast-clicking and instamatic eyes. He had no patience for strangers. He punched the horn and used foul language. Goddamn, he said. Get the lead out, he screamed. He pounded the dashboard with his fist, and in his unchanneled fury he got reckless and put us into a ditch. It happened so fast. Tires screeched and metal crunched and glass broke.

My head hit the windshield and I tried not to cry. I tried not to. The radiator hissed hot and busted. My father stopped the fast bleeding and carried me. I smelled the laundry detergent on his flannel jacket and the sweat and the gasoline, comforting and familiar. I could smell the other thing on him too, but I didn't care anymore. He scrambled us up the embankment duck-footed for traction and walked in the narrow breakdown lane against the current of oncoming traffic. Ghostly faces peered from passing cars and my father followed the painted stripe painstakingly and stuck his jaw out. Now we were the show.

I told him I was sorry.

Not your fault, he said.

He told me to keep awake. He let loose inside tears that didn't show but I felt them in his chest. I breathed deep: pin cherry and tamarack and mountain ash. He said he would really quit it this time, now that he could see how all the repercussions played out. I wanted to keep believing him, but I was tired and I closed my eyes.

SETTRIGHT ROAD

You are toast. You're in a 1962 Impala that was your dad's before he split. It's on cement blocks in the backyard. There's a heat wave going on, Indian summer. It's muggy as hell and the mosquitoes are fat and lazy and everywhere. Your mom waits tables at the BP Diner and doesn't get home until after midnight. There's a washing machine in the backyard, too, and a dog on a chain and lots of dog crap in hard piles. NRBQ is in the Dwire Lot doing its last couple sets. You fire up another doobie. The dog watches you from the end of his chain with his head cocked. It's your mom's dog and she named it Shithead—after the old man, she says, because they have the same disposition. You suck on watermelon Now and Laters with your knees against the back of the front seat. Your big brother is behind the wheel with his hands at ten and two like he's old enough to drive. He adjusts his mirrors. He moves his head to the drum solo that you can barely hear past the trees and the schoolyard and the train tracks and the long line at the beer tent. A warm breeze is like the restroom hand driers at the diner. You stuff the roach in your pocket and pretend you're riding to Virginia Beach, where your cool cousin Floyd got herpes.

You wait behind the packy in the dark with a handful of singles that smell like gasoline. The back of Fat Mike's Chevy half-ton is piled high with flattened cardboard and he's sleeping in the cab. Arnold Ogletree, who works the register on Friday and Saturday, opens the door when the coast is clear and hands you a pint of blackberry brandy, two bottles of Boone's Farm, and a twelve-pack of Budweiser. You give him the cash and a joint that is mostly oregano. You hear him lock the back door as you duck around the side of the building. Fat Mike never moved a muscle. Then you sit in the town common that isn't lit and drink your booze. The baby-blue half-dollar moon sits on top of St. Bonaventure's spire like a fixture, and you keep an eye on the police station, the firehouse, the pharmacy, and the Hot L Warren. You listen to Hank Williams coming from the jukebox in the Bloody Brook. You smell the pickle shop, the plastic shop and the tannery. You drink until you get dizzy and loud and smash empty Boone's Farm bottles on the stone borders of the wishing well. Your brother talks about the 1971 Nova in front of Gregory's Gas on 5 and 10 for when he turns sixteen. He says that's his only damn wish.

You eat Cheese Puffs and sniff model airplane glue on Danny Sternofski's mom's garage sale couch when she's pulling third shift at the plastic shop. Sterno's kid sister, who you felt up on the rocky bank of the railroad tracks after a dance, brings you meatball grinders and Jolt colas from Rogers and Brooks because you're too twisted to ride the ten-speed bikes you stole from Eaglebrook. You watch *Deputy Dawg* and *Batman* and fall asleep, then wake up with a bloody nose. Then you get to third base with Mary Anne Baggs behind the grammar school utility shed during the Labor Day barbecue. She smells like coconut suntan oil.

You break the button off her Daisy Dukes.

She says, We'd better get back.

You drink keg beer from red plastic cups and watch the old Polacks dance, drunk on vodka tonics. You tell your brother about Mary Anne Baggs' penny-colored nipples and pink nylon panties. You smoke a fatty walking home. Then you eat a whole sheet of chocolate chip cookies your mother had baked for her new boyfriend from the Shutesbury Rod and Gun Club. You piss in a two-liter plastic Coke bottle, pass out on the floor.

The farmer who owns the land around Red Rock has put up Keep Out signs because some college kid from Amherst drowned himself and his parents got a lawyer from Springfield and sued. You don't keep out, though, and your brother says if the old coot comes down with his pepper gun you'd better be ready to swim to Stillwater Bridge. You smoke a fat one with Tony Waznieski by the rope swing and blow up Michelob bottles with firecrackers. Later the Big Wazoo, as you call him, lays a patch of rubber about two inches thick because he's selling his 1970 Charger since he's joining the Army. You cheer and watch the heat in translucent strip-of-bacon shapes coming off the blacktop of North River Road. You sit on towels in the backseat and kill a warm pint of Southern Comfort that Waz keeps in a speaker hole cut with a razor.

There's a bonfire at Hoosac's. You're out of your tits when you hear about the crash. It sounds like your mom's 1974 Comet. She'll have a fit. She doesn't even let your brother practice with her car because of the pickup he stole with Lester Little, but she's over to the Seven O's and he had an extra key made at Elder Lumber when she was napping. You ride by in the back of a police cruiser and blow chunks when you see it. You know right away he's really toast this time.

It's horseshoed around a hundred-year-old maple and the windshield ripples outward from where his head hit, like pond water disturbed by a stone. They use the Jaws of Life to pull him free and the torn metal roof is the mouth of some angry backwoods brute with sharp and misshapen silver teeth glinting and grinning, spitting your busted brother into the hands of men who cannot save him. The fat tires of the boxy refrigerator-white rescue vehicle hurry and crunch over shards of glass that are a million fallen stars and you wish on every one of them. Then sweaty men in muddy boots yell instructions at the driver of the yellow wrecker from Fisher's Garage and as you pass they all look up, shake their heads, and say he never felt a thing.

At Cooley Dick in Hamp he's gone but for a machine, and your mom is there with her stained apron and she looks at you like you put that tree there. Nobody says anything except her new boyfriend from the Rod and Gun who calls you a waste. The halls smell like Pine-Sol and those little plastic packs of grape jelly from the first-floor cafeteria. They unplug the machine the next day and everybody cries at the funeral. His hair is wrong and his clothes are wrong and one side of his face is a peach that has been dropped. You sit outside on the curb and swat at hungry horseflies and look at limousines. Then you sit in church. They bury your brother on Thayer Road across from Boron's Market. They stick him in the ground two stones down from Robert Hawk Wilson and right across from Eugene Canning's mother. Four old townies use straps and metal bars and globs of black machine grease to drop the handsome box into the fresh-dug dirt. The sun shivers in the sky like a reflection of itself in a slow-moving current.

The green leaves of Olzewski's corn scratch the skin on your arms. After the corn comes the trees and the hill and then the river. The path to Red Rock is worn and narrow and your brother is behind you. Your shadows consolidate in the smoky dirt, like you aren't two separate people anymore, like he's becoming the strong blond part of you. The water is clear and rushing and three or four fish are facing upriver, sleepily feeding in the drift. You take off your T-shirts and jeans and boots and pile them behind a buttonball stump. An eddy chug-a-lugs. You're under and you push downriver, past stones and licorice-quick eels, and then come up for air a few short strokes from the red rock. Sitting on top the sun dries your hair and deciduous leaves whisper secrets. Mapleseed helicopters soundlessly descend into calm pockets. Some strange daddy-long-legs panics and scampers, dances on the surface. Alone together one last time but for the echo of a carpenter's hammer. You're the one who's going to notice it most, your brother says. In the distance, Mount Toby is orange and red and yellow, always most glorious just before dying.

NICE SLEEP

Sideways rain hit the aluminum sides of the double-wide like fistfuls of pebbles. The green couch was ripped. Water was boiling for tea. I heard it going over the sides of the red kettle and onto the electric burner. I put an old bag of Orange Pekoe and a cube of sugar in the one cup she hadn't broken and burned my finger a bit on the black handle of the kettle, held it under the tap until it went away. We were out of milk. She didn't want to be alone. I brought it to her like that, with a paper napkin and a spoon.

Go get my medicine you little shit, she said, and she told me which ones and I brought them and she tilted her head back to swallow each pill one at a time. Her room was dark. Her room smelled like fish. Now get away from me you little shit, she said. I went back to watch television.

It was four in the morning but I didn't have to get up for school anymore. She didn't let me go to school. She said if she let me out of her sight they'd take me away forever this time. She said she loved me more than life.

Go put some clothes on, she said. I woke up and she was standing there and she told me to get dressed. I'd been sleeping on the green couch, in my underpants and a sweater that smelled like the tire from the trunk of the Buick we used to live in. It was daytime now. The television was still on and she shut it off.

It was cold. I was cold. The trailer was cold because we didn't pay for oil and Chet Templeton with the wooden leg who owned the White Birch Campgrounds shut off the generator, and I could see my breath. She was in the kitchenette when I was ready except for my shoes in my hand and she looked at me for a minute before she said anything. Then she spoke.

Get the fuck out, she said. Leave me alone. Get fucking lost and don't ever come back. If it wasn't for you, she said, I could drive a red sports car.

So I got Richard Peach from four trailers down and we went to look at the dogs. Malek was the auto mechanic and dogcatcher and Richard Peach said Malek would shoot dogs after ten days. And the crazies even sooner. He said he took them out back by the oil drums and put one right in their brains. Richard Peach said if he saw it once he saw it a million times. He said that they were better off dead anyhow because they didn't have anything to live for. It was just a matter of putting them out of their misery. He said Malek did it for free because he took pleasure in it. All he did was charge for ammo. There was a fat black and grey Keeshond at the end of a greasy rope, and he barked and charged and his stomach moved from side to side just like pudding would. Salty foam boiled over his blue gums. We ran when Malek saw us. He came around the side of the garage with a shovel over his shoulder and a shotgun that was longer than me. He hollered, and we cut across the potato fields behind his place and walked when we got to the old drive-in movie theater. The ground was hard with frost. I shivered and Richard Peach said it was colder than a witch's tit. He said we'd sure see some snow in a couple three weeks.

———

I didn't get home until dark and after I knocked for a while she un-locked the door. How could you leave me alone like that, she said. She was on the green couch with a blanket and the telephone and a pink roll of toilet paper. She hit me on top of the head with the phone. You don't even care, she said. The apple doesn't fall far from the tree after all.

I washed up for bed and she hit me in the face with both ends of the red flashlight we kept for emergencies until my left eye wouldn't open. She told me to go to my room. Go to your room, you little shit.

I fell asleep and woke up and she was standing right there and it was dark. She told me that she couldn't take it anymore and I had to go away. For good this time, she said. Life is hard enough without you.

Rain came down like curtains. If we don't make rent we're going to get evicted again, my mother said. We sat in the Buick in front of the Bloody Brook Bar on North Main. She tapped the gas three times and turned the ignition off fast so the engine wouldn't diesel. She stared at the pine air freshener that dangled from the volume knob on the AM radio that didn't work anymore. Then she looked at the door to the Bloody Brook. I hope there's a man in there with some scratch, she said. Then she slapped me until her hand got tired. Stay put, little fucker, she said. Get in back and take a nap why don't you.

She checked herself in the rearview, stretched the neck band of her T-shirt to rub an invisible film from her teeth, smoothed out her eyebrows with fingertips of spittle. She rolled the window down, opened the door with the outside handle, rolled the window up, got out and closed the door with the jut of her hip. She held a chamois over her head so her makeup wouldn't run in the rain. Jukebox music poured out of the bar, filled me like oxygen.

———

We made rent and the next day the wind blew so hard they gave it a woman's name and told us to stay indoors. Chet came around with plywood and plastic and ten-penny nails. He stood on an overturned bucket and used a hammer with a blue rubber handle. He leaned on his good leg, made a lot of noise, looked at me like I was something bad, then left. I slept on the green couch.

If I can't have him then nobody can, my mother said. I kept my eyes shut. But I could feel her standing over me with something or somebody else, whispering. It was dark. It was cold. The night was howling, a sooty brute, and in the light of the storm her face looked like it was of the stuff they forged cutlery from. Have a nice sleep, boy, she said. But don't expect to wake up.

BARNYARD

He had a scarecrow beard that seemed to grow from everywhere on his face and he moved across the yard real slow like some specter. Some straw-filled specter. He stepped over the rust-pocked chrome bumper of an old American car and made his way to the brown-boarded tobacco barn. The early morning mist wrapped itself around him like a vestment. Like an old robe. There were chickens and dogs and pigs in the yard and he spit yellow at them and they parted to let him pass.

A small squalid face pushed pale against the screen door and called out. He stopped and cursed and turned. Hell you want Chance, he said. A waist-high boy ran out of the house and jumped the three porch steps, his swiftspindle legs constantly moving until he caught up to the man. I want to help you, Dad, he said. The man put his hand in the boy's hair and they went together to the barn. The boy was naked but for a tiny pair of unlaced work boots. He picked up a weeping willow stick and dragged it in the dirt at his side and waved it at the chickens and poked it at the dogs and pigs that swarmed around him. He made noises at them too and they licked and pecked and nudged him, the dirty boy, until he giggled, but it was empty of joy. Inside the barn was dark like a tomb and rats scurried along the rafters and wooden beams. There were cats, too, that killed the fat rats and hissed and hid in dark corners. The man set his son on an overturned grain barrel and told him to stay put. Stay you put now, boy, he said, and let me do this here.

He built his wife a handsome box because she didn't like what was in the catalogs. He banged nails with a blue-handle hammer. He cut pine board with an angry triangle-tooth ripsaw. He smoothed it with decreasing grits of sandpaper. He finished it with linseed oil and lined it with crushed velvet. She wanted to die in her wedding dress. The boy remained, potbellied and quiet.

Chance hadn't seen his mother in eighty days. She was sick and stayed in her room. She hacked blood into a white handkerchief or an old T-shirt. If you go near her then you'll get it too, his father said. The boy listened, obeyed. He watched his father from his woody perch. The man worked on the stubby end of a cigar and put his right foot on a concrete block for support. The smoke rose up and around his face, carried bits of his warbled soul up into the abyss of ceiling beams and spider webs where it lingered. When he finished smoking the cigar he chewed it, rolled it across his lower lip, then spit it against the wall where it clung like a living thing.

They got flowers and cards and they placed her in the ground on a day that was rainy. They kept a clipping from the paper and a copy of the Lord's prayer. The rain and the wind turned the umbrellas inside out and the whole thing didn't take long because the limo was by the hour. It had a maroon interior and a minibar and a television screen that didn't come on because that was extra. The driver had dandruff on the shoulders of his suitcoat. There was a plastic window between the front and back that slid open and closed. It wasn't like being in a car at all or a pickup truck. It wasn't bumpy or noisy or uncomfortable either. There was leg room for everybody and nobody had to sit up straight or lean their arm out the window. They went from the church to the graveyard and back to the church where they had left their vehicles.

The men stood around smoking cigarettes and talking to the limo driver, who smoked too. They admired the limo. The women waited by the cars and pickup trucks and smoked and talked about the flower arrangements that the rain, which had let up for a minute but was forecast through the weekend, would ruin. The men undid their ties and unbuttoned their shirts, and the women stood easier in bare feet than in the dress shoes they now held in their hands. Then the limo was gone because the driver was on the clock and the church was filling up for another service for somebody else who went and died. And the pastor who did most everything, even emptied the trash and fixed the toilet, asked them to please remove the cars and pickup trucks from the parking lot. He shook their hands and passed around a shiny silver flask. Chance's father crouched down so he was eye level with his son.

Go with Tanti for a little while, he said. I just need to be alone.

Tanti smelled like Maker's Mark. She took her teeth out at night and put them in a drinking glass. Around the house she wore big pink slippers that she called her puppies. Tanti was a Bruins fan. She said Bobby Orr should be the mayor. She watched hockey on her black-and-white television. She listened to games on the radio at the kitchen table. Tanti was retired from the town and lived in a shack on a hill all by herself. She caused a scene at Wolfie's last Thanksgiving and Chance's father went to wait in his pickup in the parking lot. She had a bathtub but not a shower and she let him stay in there for as long as he wanted. She had a hundred Hummel figurines that she warned him away from because they were going to be worth a lot of money someday. He broke the head off a porcelain boy with a sheep and she used crazy glue to stick it back on. Tanti always read the newspaper to see who else had died.

She kept Kleenex rolled up in the sleeve of her shirt. She had a friend named Mr. Kenny who worked for Lipton and gave her Cup-a-Soup by the case. He had a son named Dougie Kenny who Chance shot with a water pistol because he was retarded. Tanti told Chance to leave him alone because he couldn't help the way he was. She told him to stay off the old firehouse roof next door. She told him to stop throwing rocks at cars on Parker Street. She told him to be home before dark. She gave him money to go to the candy store across the park, where he got a grape-flavor lollipop. She gave him money to go to the five and dime on Bernie Avenue so he wouldn't steal toys anymore. Tanti didn't know how to drive a car. She wore a wig that was blonde. She said Bing Crosby was her favorite. She danced drunk around the living room and sang songs from Bobby Vinton until she got tired. Then she went to sleep on the hardwood floor.

The wind was blowing awful bad in the barnyard. I was used to her being dead but it was different without the boy. Everything was dried up now. It didn't matter. Our mulberry was black and skinny and grabbing at me with a million twistjointed arms. I sat with my feet planted in Sugarloaf Street and a Peterbilt had business at the pickle shop. It downshifted on the railroad tracks and dropped heads of cabbage into the street that bounced and rolled around like heads of cabbage do. I smelled them and the fresh-cut pulpwood from the lumberyard across the river. Then I locked myself in the cellar with a stack of Playboys and a 1.75-liter bottle of Gordon's and a small-caliber

*handgun. I kept all that stashed in a hole in the sheetrock.
I asked God why and waited for an answer, listened to the
high-pitched hum of the fridge that stored last year's veni-
son, and put my cheek to the cement that was colder than
a froze-over pond.*

CUT ME IN PIECES
AND HIDE

The sky outside my window was wide and white. Birds flew from a strange summer fog, passed before me and smacked into the silence again. My mother was disappearing. She told me I was a bastard. She hit me with the vacuum cleaner. When she stopped I got up from the floor and ran away. I went to the waterfall near Bardwell's Ferry that everybody called the fork. I stayed until a cool moon illuminated the valley and I knew she had gone into her room to die a little more.

Then I knocked on her window until she unlocked the front door and studied me like a barn cat crazed with hunger. Get your ass in here, she said. Her hybrid meds were cocktailing to strike a chemical balance in her perpetually seesaw brain. Her faraway eyes focused on an imprecise point over my left shoulder. She told me she called the police switchboard because she thought maybe I got hit by a car or stuck in the swamp or taken away by a man with bad skin in a white panel truck. She always imposed her recurring nightmares on me. She meant to protect me.

You are my life, she said. Don't ever leave me again.

We went to her bed and hugged. She put her arms around me so I could see the train-track scars that made me queasy from where she especially liked to kill herself. Then I wasn't really sleeping anymore and I heard her walking up and down the hall. She was off-kilter again and getting more so by the minute. I observed her discreetly with my one good eye and it was true she was a haunt already in her white T-shirt and her white legs and her arms and her white face.

In the morning I went to the cemetery on Stanislaus Street, which was like a park. There was a pond with a red bridge slicing it in half and cattails at one end. There were snapping turtles. I smashed bullfrogs with sticks. I sneaked up on them and hit them hard. I threw them into the air so they landed on the blacktop with a sound like a single wet clap. And when Tommy Zagrodnik and Rocky Morales showed up we played smear the queer. I spit bubble-gum into Tommy's hair and slapped him with both hands until his teeth bled, and Rocky told his grandmother, who was scared of me. She wouldn't let them play with me anymore, so I chased ducks that were green and gray. I crawled up behind them pretending to be a soldier, keeping my head down to avoid imaginary barbed wire and make-believe sniper fire. I jumped to my feet with abusive whoops of chaos and they scrambled down the mud-slick bank and glided easily away from the danger that had become such a fundamental part of me.

After hitchhiking 116 and 91 to the Holyoke Mall, I looked at black-light posters and talked to the talking parrots near the wishing well. I took a penny from the water and closed my eyes. Then I returned the copper embodiment of hope to its original fluid jurisdiction, generating ripples outward as it penetrated the glassy surface, sinking side to side to the bottom like a falling feather. I didn't know for sure if it worked like that but hoped it did; I'd wished my mother finally dead, but not in a hateful way. More for her than me. By her own account she was not well-suited among the living. Then I sat by the Orange Julius booth just to smell them. The girl behind the counter wore a paper hat and vest. She chopped oranges and strawberries and she crushed big bags of ice. She didn't look at me, not one time, and I didn't really blame her.

I stayed in the atrium too long because it was hot outside and the blue-uniformed security guard kept an eye on me. His face was dark and bumpy as a chestnut. He talked into his radio. He wore black boots and fingered his baton. He stopped watching me to help a woman with a baby, and I stole a candy bar from the drugstore and left with it stuffed inside my pants.

The front door opened again. You little bastard, she said. She broke everything in the kitchen all over the floor and made me watch. Plates. Glasses. Bowls. The blender. A vase. A jar where we used to keep colorful pasta when things weren't that bad. The toaster right out of the wall. Then she hit me with her wrists, which hardly hurt anymore because she was shrinking so small. Smaller than me. Then she told me to get a broom and clean up the mess that I made. I swept it against a cardboard scrap and put it in the trash. She was tired because of what I had just put her through so I apologized. She swallowed blue pills with water. I watched *The Wild Wild West*. She covered her legs with a thin afghan and appeared to struggle mightily as it gobbled her up.

And I knew she didn't stand a chance anymore.

Not in this life.

Then she woke up and looked at me and opened her mouth and the words came out.

Cut me, she said. Cut me in pieces and hide.

Then a muted sound that I sorted from the others and even the sound of my own beating heart, the distant yelps of a mange-coat coyote conspiring with the northeast wind, slicing the silence and signaling some ancient distress known to nature, purveying a vague call to arms.

NUTS

Aunt Rose told me she made a nice meatloaf. Come and eat, she said. It was the first of June, and Yaz and Fisk and the Boston Red Sox were on the radio. She lived in a green house on Oak Street in Indian Orchard. She told me I ate like Georgie Flynn from when she was a girl about my age. Aunt Rose was old and she let me stay up late so I could watch James Bond in *The Man with the Golden Gun* and dunk lemon-cream Girl Scout cookies in a big cup of cold milk.

The next day was hot. Aunt Rose told me she hated the heat. She sat in the kitchen with a fan from the five-and-dime blowing on her and a glass of what she liked to call iced tea. She talked into the yellow telephone, mostly about the godforsaken weather, and I listened for a while then went out on the back porch. Stanley Bailey next door was riding his lawn mower. It was green and he was fat and red, and he drove around the trees in his yard. He wouldn't cut Aunt Rose's grass because he thought she was nuts. You're all nuts, he said.

My mother called from the funny farm in Tewksbury, Fridays after supper. She asked if Aunt Rose was drunk. Are you being a good boy, she said. She told me it was a decent place but it wasn't actually a farm. It had a pond and trees like a cemetery. And there were ducks. And she made a leather belt with my name on it. I asked if she was feeling better. My mother told me I could visit. I asked how long until she was normal again and she told me she didn't know.

I handed the phone to Aunt Rose and she touched my head and told my mother I was a good boy. Then her lips got so thin her mouth looked like a deep razor cut on the wrist that moment before the blood surfaces. He's my good boy, she said. Then she got quiet while my mother made the usual cruel accusations. Aunt Rose cried and rubbed her eyes and told me it was the pollen. Goddamn the hay fever, she said. She told me if the humidity didn't kill her then the pollen sure would. She made iced tea in the pantry. She got the squat dark bottle of Canadian Mist down from the top shelf and sat on the step stool to catch her breath. She drank and said, Ahhhh. She said, That's much better.

The setting sun was melting butter, a wide sky brushstroked mango backdropping split-level houses and storefronts and the solitary spire of St. Matthew's Church. Then it got dark enough for streetlights and I threw crabapples from Aunt Rose's tree into Stanley Bailey's yard. I threw them by the handful. I could still smell the grass he cut. My arms itched from mosquitoes because Aunt Rose forgot to put bug spray on me. She called out the window for me to come inside and we had tapioca pudding that she burned so it formed a brown skin. I ate two bowlfuls. She fell asleep on the couch and snored and I turned the television loud and louder. The temperature was unforgiving even at night, a brutal and humid summer. Aunt Rose had the fan in the room with us and I aimed it at her. She didn't wake up. I made her wig blow off.

Stanley Bailey told Aunt Rose I was throwing crabapples at his yard. I heard him from the window. Aunt Rose told him he was a sonofabitch and to get off her property. I'll call the police. Ought to be ashamed. Picking on the boy. He left and she repeated my name again and again and I ran away to where Oak Street ended in a tree line. I chucked rocks at the shut-down Chapman Valve Company where Aunt Rose kept books for twenty-six years. It was a brick building that took up two square blocks. There was no more glass to break and there were boards where all the windows used to be. There was spray paint on the walls that plugged the Maniac Latin Hoods. I went home when the moon was white as a pillow and the shape of that thing on the bottom third of my thumb nail and Aunt Rose made me a toasted peanut butter and jam sandwich and chocolate-flavor milk. She told me she didn't know what to do when I acted up like that. She told me I was going to give her a coronary. Is that what you want, she said.

I told my mother about running away. My mother asked what happened and I told her about the crabapples and she said Stanley Bailey has no balls. Put her on the phone.

I didn't mean for Aunt Rose to get in trouble. Then we listened to the game. I drank ginger ale with ice cubes and a cherry. Aunt Rose let me use a crazy straw with a blue stripe. She told me she'd been to Fenway Park. She told me about the wall they called the Green Monster and the smell of French fries. Maybe we can take a Greyhound bus. We can get hot dogs and grape slushies, she said. She told me she'd buy me a cap. Something fun for once, she said.

I drew pictures on the construction paper from Johnson's Books that Aunt Rose kept by the phone. I used the Crayola set I got for my birthday. I drew pictures of Jim Rice hitting home runs and Rick Burleson number seven and Stanley Bailey with a penis and no balls. I drew a picture of my mother feeding a wire coat hanger through her strawberry-shaped heart. The Yankees won after ten innings and Aunt Rose let me go to bed without brushing my teeth. I slept in the room where Nana died, and the wind outside was surely her unsettled spirit lingering.

———

Aunt Rose gave me the funnies from the Springfield Union. She put her glasses on and told me about sports. And there was a summer storm coming down the valley. We were getting rain. Cats and dogs, she said. She knew the day before because her knees hurt. She told me not to get old. She told me arthritis would be the death of her, and I asked her when my mother was going to get discharged, and she took a long sip of her drink and told me she didn't know. Your mother's awful sick. She needs help. Aunt Rose did the crossword puzzle and I watched some wrongful god's tears in puddles on Oak Street. Drops fat as planets descended like the end of the world.

Then I counted my heartbeats between thunder and lightning. One-one thousand, two-one thousand, three…

I counted it getting closer. My mother didn't call. Aunt Rose told me to take a bath because somebody was coming. She cut my hair with black-handle scissors she kept on the kitchen table. She told me my mother wouldn't mind. Oh, she'll never even know, she said. The lady's name was Miss McGee and she told me I had a lawyer. She asked questions. Aunt Rose talked for a while and I wanted to go outside. It's not because your mother doesn't love you, she said. It's not your fault, she said. Miss McGee drank a glass of tap water. I could hear the ice cubes go pop, pop, pop. Now we need to find a place for you to live, she said. She had a clipboard.

Aunt Rose showed her the pictures I made. She told Miss McGee she was too old for all this. She told me she was sorry. My poor boy. Miss McGee told Aunt Rose they would determine the most suitable situation. Another ice cube from her drink popped. I told her I didn't want to go anywhere else. Then I stood up and walked outside and they followed me and I stopped right at the edge of Stanley Bailey's yard. There was a break in the storm and he was cleaning his gutters from a tall aluminum ladder and he was fat and red, and he looked at me like I was nuts.

I WON'T WEAR BLACK

Red is my big brother and can kick anybody's ass. They call him that because that's the color his face turns when he's mad. We're sitting on the hood of our mother's brown Ford Pinto in front of the apartment building where we live with mostly niggers and spics. The sun is hot and the metal of the car is hot too. There's a public pool across the street but we're not allowed anymore because I pushed Matthew Ackerman into the deep end so we all could watch him drown.

Red is smoking a cigarette and he won't let me have any because I'm too young. He's only a year older, and he stole them from the store on the corner of Parker Street and Walnut. He also lifted a liter of Coke, and it's ice cold. I drink it too fast and so it looks like I'm crying.

Gary Foster comes over to fuck with us and Red puts the cigarette out in his eye. Gary cries for real and runs home to tell his fat fucking parents. Red laughs out loud and I do too. That was my last goddamn cigarette, he says, trying to sound crazy like Uncle Quick. Then our mother sticks her head out the window and sees us. She twists up her face like a mask. You little cocksuckers, she says. Inside the apartment she comes at us hard with hands and elbows. My brother protects me until my mother gets tired and stops, leans against the doorframe, coughs and says she can't take it anymore.

She's going to put us on a Greyhound to our father, that no good sonofabitch.

I hope it crashes into a mountain, she says.

I won't go to your funeral.

I won't even wear black.

FLUNKY

I sniffed model airplane glue with Walter while his mom waited tables at HoJo's. His kid sister smelled like soap. She said she was sick and stayed home from school. I gave her money from my uncle's wallet so she'd ride to the center of town on her bike with the basket to get us a family-size bag of ranch-flavored Doritos and two one-liter bottles of Pepsi. Mighty Mouse was flying over cartoon skyscrapers. We watched him on the black-and-white television that had rolled-up aluminum foil as an antenna. A train went by on the tracks right outside the house and from the couch we saw it pass in dark kitchen-window-size squares. When the cabinets stopped rattling Walter said, Fifteen cars. When we couldn't even hear it anymore because it already went under the dry bridge past Elder Lumber I told him I counted seventeen. He said he hated that I always had to have the last word. He punched me in the shoulder and said I always had to be right. A fat black fly tried to escape through the screen part of the side door. It buzzed and bounced against the cat-scratched screen, buzzed and bounced trying like hell to get out.

The yellow telephone erupted like a fire drill. It was on the chipped pink tile floor of the bathroom, where Walter's mom talked in a hushed whiskey voice from the edge of the clawfoot tub between cigarette drags, late at night when she thought everybody was asleep. I rubbed my eyes and my head where it hurt from the glue hangover and Walter woke up too.

Don't answer it, he said. It's probably the school.

Then my nose started to bleed and I filled my nostrils with Kleenex. From the big-numbered clock hanging crooked from a nail on the wall I could see it was the beginning of fourth period. We'd left right after homeroom, walked across the parking lot and past the weed-cracked tennis courts and through the softball field and the old Dwire Lot to the house that Walter's mom rented. Walter's kid sister, a year behind us, was in eighth grade and she had good marks and blue ribbons from 4-H and a fancy letter from the board of education saying she could spell better than anybody in Franklin County. Walter's mom called Kayla her last hope.

I heard Kayla put the kickstand down on her bike and take hold of the plastic bag from Rogers and Brooks. I heard her come in, the side door banging inside the frame as she jiggled it shut all the way. Walter went into his bedroom and came back with a pack of EZ-Wider and the Sucrets tin where he kept the dope he bought from Jimmy Warfield's father. He told Kayla to get lost, go do homework, and he licked his index fingers and thumbs and rolled a fat one in his lap. We took a few hits and ate the Doritos and I drank my Pepsi. Batman and Robin were on the television. The fly was bouncing off the screen door again and the plastic clock was ticking and the wind outside was brushing a weeping willow branch against the vinyl siding of the house. The telephone rang four and a half times. We've got to get out of here, somebody on the television said. Walter was breathing through his nose and making snoring sounds and when I looked at him the ends of his fingers were Dorito orange and all around his mouth was Dorito orange and the plastic one-liter Pepsi bottle was unopened between his legs.

I heard Kayla in her room with the door mostly shut listening to Bryan Adams on Walter's old boom box and turning the pages of a magazine. I pushed the door open with my big toe and the rusty hinge creaked. She was lying face down on her bed that looked like a little girl's bed. She was wearing somebody's old Calvin Kleins from the hand-me-down store in Northampton and a three-quarter sleeve REO Speedwagon concert T-shirt. I told her that she smelled like Dove soap and she let me come in and sit on the bed with her. We made out and I took her shirt and bra off and dropped them on the sticky hardwood floor. Then she stood up and locked her door and took her jeans and panties off. She told me I made her feel beautiful and grown up and somehow unconnected to anything. I said some other things that I knew she wanted to hear and after a short while she took my clothes off.

Make sure you take it out this time, she said.

The greenish paint was flaking off the plaster walls of her room. Dark spots of mildew on the south one that faced out over the front yard. We smoked some old Marlboro lights she got from the dresser in her mom's room and she said her mom would kill her if she found out. She said her mom put too much pressure on her to be perfect. She told me I was lucky not to have anybody to tell me what to do and I told her more lies about my feelings and shit to hush her up, and blew smoke rings that drifted up to the bowl of the dead-moth-filled ceiling light. I listened to the wind outside go around the house and from her window I watched it make mini tornadoes of raked maple leaves in the yard and dirt and driveway. The rain came straight down and then the wind turned it sideways for a while. Oh fuck, the windows, Kayla said, and put her jeans and shirt on and pushed her underwear under the bed with her foot. She closed her window against the rain and I heard her going through all the rooms, closing windows while I got dressed.

———

Walter woke up and looked at me. Where the hell'd you go to, he said.

I told him it was raining. There was a game show on the television. Walter told his kid sister to leave the window in the living room open because we wanted to fire up another doobie. She looked right at me, flipped me the bird, went into her room, and slammed the door.

What's up her ass, Walter said.

I shrugged.

We took a couple hits and tried to blow the smoke toward the window so his mom wouldn't smell it when she got home. We didn't know any answers to the game show questions but there was only one other channel and it didn't come in during rain.

The one good headlight lit the room up for a few seconds when Walter's mom turned into the driveway from Stage Road. Her car hiccupped and sputtered as she killed the engine. I heard Kayla spray Lysol and open her bedroom door a few inches. Walter's mom came in holding a *Recorder* over her head and a paper bag against her hip. Cats and dogs out there, she said.

Kayla boiled water for macaroni and cheese, chopped hot dogs, buttered slices of stale white bread. Walter's mom served iceberg lettuce that was brown around the edges with a mayonnaise and ketchup dressing that I watched her mix with a fork. Then she brought our dinners on paper plates to the couch. Walter's mom took a shower and said she was going to be late. It's poker night, she said, so it could be a big tip night. I can't afford to be late again. On her way out the door she jerked her thumb toward Walter and me and told Kayla, Stay away from the flunkies. I don't want them two losers rubbing off on you, she said.

Walter nudged me in the ribs and I laughed out loud.

———

We drank vodka right from the bottle I took from my uncle who had temporary custody. Kayla smoked one of her mom's cigarettes. Walter passed out again and Kayla told me she made an appointment with Nurse Harper for between study hall and History on Wednesday. The radio played a block of Def Leppard. She made a face when she put the bottle to her lips but tilted her head back and gargled the vodka like Listerine and eventually swallowed it. She went on to say that Nurse Harper was going to give her the results of a test. She told me that she already pissed on one from the pharmacy and it was positive. Kayla was leaning on her elbow and trying to find something in my face that was not there and I took a long snort so I could close my eyes. She cried and said my name to bring me back, but the wind outside was the familiar ghost of something long since dead. Rain came down in big drops that sounded to me like footsteps.

MOON OR HEAVEN

This was when my father died.

My grandmother sat on the porch. A foldout chair. A tall drink. A telescope on a three-legged stand. She watched tankers going to Boston. Hauling sugar. Automobiles. Coffee beans. Out past No Name Island. Way past. She sipped. The sun was unbreakable. My grandfather opened the screen door with his big toe and unfolded the umbrella so she wouldn't cook. Doctor's orders. Not too much sun. Not after the stroke in the basement that left her twitching in a puddle of herself by the washing machine. Concussion. Unconscious. Mrs. Sturtevant went down there with a load of whites and found her three hours later.

But drinking was all right. In moderation. He mixed them in the kitchen—vodka and cranberry, whiskey and ginger. He didn't say a word to her and she didn't acknowledge his efforts. He slipped back inside to watch baseball. She adjusted the telescope with her good hand and saw us making our way down the beach. Past the Levitt's. The Magnolia Bath and Tennis Club where the rich teenagers went. The Mongeon's volleyball net. We knew she was watching. It was understood. That's all she had left.

Pan right. Pick target. Focus.

Seaweed on the beach was a collection of brown bodies and it smelled dead and rotten and we could hear fat horseflies around it black and mad and buzzing like wires. Beer bottles. Bottle rockets. A pair of sunglasses. We walked through it with no shoes and no shirts and chucked handfuls at each other and chased the clear-winged devils. There was a boulder at the west end that was our spaceship. At the foot of the rocky ring of the cove. Pricker bushes. Poison ivy. Private signs. The haunted house. Cunt Cave, where Cousin Dennis got his head stuck. The craft loomed out of the sand like a dream and we sat in the seats that seemed to have been carved for us by a god often negligent. It took us everywhere and anywhere. My father sat on top because he was the captain and said he could see the harbor. Lobster boats. Catamarans. Twenty-five-foot whalers. I sat below, on a ledge. I could see him. Lean. Freckled. Father strong.

Where are we going this time, I asked.

Mars, he said. Jupiter. The moon. Wherever, he said. It don't matter. Jump out when the aliens get here.

We had traveled far. Light years. Solar systems. Galaxies. I told him to be sure and tell me when. An old Irish Setter named Ajax bounded around us snapping his frothy jaws at nothing. Or everything. Barking. Red dog collar. Tags like a little bell signaling his canine frenzy. Green-gray tennis ball. Then the captain told me to close my eyes and look at the moon. Shiny quarter dollar. Snow cone.

It's getting closer, he said. We're almost there.

I told him I could tell. I told him I wasn't retarded. I closed my eyes just like he instructed and I could feel the earth behind me and the wind sounded like waves in the Atlantic Ocean and seagulls screaming for bloody chum.

Get ready to jump, he said.

So I jumped and rolled like he taught me in the sand, throwing elbows and knees at the Martians or whoever and cried for help.

Helpless. Small. I kept my eyes closed because I didn't want to see them because he told me they were horrible. Hairy. Angry. Yellow-fanged.

I'll save you, he said. He pulled them off me. The beasts. The bastards. Die, he yelled. Die you beasts. You bastards.

He killed two with a stick, drowned three in the sea, brained one with a brick. He told me so. I felt him there and smelled his breath. Southern Comfort and cigarettes. When I opened my eyes he was chasing the last one away. The beast was wild and orange-woolly and snapping at flies. My arm was bleeding. Tooth marks. Ripped skin. The captain rubbed mud on me that worked like medicine. I was almost a goner, he told me. Dead. Kicked the bucket. Passed away. Lucky for you I was around. He washed me in a salty eddy that swirled. Move it like this, he showed me. Like this, and he did it. You're going to be all right, he told me. You'll live to see another day.

He didn't mention alone.

Scared.

Unprotected.

Abandoned.

My grandfather folded the umbrella, closed the tripod telescope. Propped it in the living room. Time to pack it in, he said. That's all she wrote. Goodnight, Irene. He helped my grandmother stand up. Dusk settled on the horizon like dust on a windowsill. Thick. Clinging. Storm clouds formed a heavy blanket thrown over Magnolia. She clutched her drink against her breast in her good hand that worked like a claw. Thunder was a cherry bomb bursting beyond a charcoal haze. A zigzag of electricity whipsawed its way groundward. Crack. Snap. And another. She sobbed. Shivered. He was oblivious—how could he have known—and made her another drink. A nightcap. One for the road, he said. He helped her into bed. Don't worry, he said. They're good boys and always make it home. He waited up for what he thought would be both of us with the television lighting up his face in blue flashes. *Archie Bunker. Mork and Mindy. M.A.S.H.*

If the stroke hadn't taken words from my grandmother she might've told him. Because I think she knew. I think she learned new ways of knowing once her sickness took over. This came to me later, too late. With her eye against the world, she had watched the green leaves of cattails scratch the skin on our arms. The path from the beach to the Swan Pond was worn and narrow. My father was disappearing. She checked focus. Maybe a smudge on the lense. Spittle. This is what she saw. Then the treeline obscured her view. We skinny dipped. Bare ass. Cool. Big kids smoking cigarettes across the way. Marlboro. Keeping an eye on us. Plotting. Maybe. An omen. A warning sign. But where will you end up, I said. The moon, he said. Or heaven. Wherever.

STAY WHERE YOU ARE

Snow falling was flakes of old paint and our room at the Hot L Warren was cold. This is no way to live, my mother said. Then she gave
me food stamps to use for her medicine at the Frontier Pharmacy on
Main Street and Sugarloaf.

Bobby Popovic, behind the counter with the spots on his face
and the wet hair said, No way. Tell her forget it, he said. Not this
time. Not anymore.

She waited outside in the tan 1962 Chevy Bel Air that had a
busted driver-side headlight and rust patches that were eating away
at the car like an apricoty cancer. The night was dark and cold and
the moon was a perfect Carl Yaz pop fly from summer. She watched
through the glass door that had a cowbell on the handle that would
ring when it opened. Bobby Popovic handed it back to me all rolled
up like I'd had it in my pocket. Go on and beat it, kid, he said.

But she was waiting outside. I was going to be in trouble. She really needed her medicine this time and I didn't have to look because I
knew she was watching from the car, leaning over the steering wheel,
drumming the dashboard with her press-on fingernails, breathing
short puffs you could see like her spirit slow-leaking.

I didn't move from the black-speckled Formica countertop that
came up to my chin, terribly aware that the only thing between me

and her rage was the stretch of cigarette-scarred carpet that flanked the stools that lined the soda fountain. And the slightest indication of failure on my part would bring her in here for one of her scenes. So I didn't move a muscle and the world around me stayed oblivious to my predicament. The smell of black coffee was so strong it triggered my other senses too. Kielbasa from Pekarski's off 116 in Conway sizzled on the grill. Dutch Syska smoked a Swisher Sweet and ate a cheeseburger with pickled onions. The radio near the frappe machine played a polka from the station in Northampton. Fat Mike squirted ketchup onto steak-cut French fries one at a time. Moe Sadoski spit Beechnut chewing tobacco juice into a Styrofoam cup and played cards by himself in the booth that was supposed to be for two or more. The toaster popped a couple slices of rye for Bubba Hubboch's BLT. Pat Bismo under her chemical-blue beehive shook a can of Reddi-Wip with one hand and with the other poured a hot chocolate for Joey Hostrop, who drove the snow plow during storms. Then the red and white can hissed its final sweet kiss and Pat tossed it into the trash can near the cash register.

Billy, the owner, came from around back where I could hear *It's a Wonderful Life* on the television, and he had on a big white shirt with short sleeves and big white buttons. He folded his furry arms across his belly, the back of them spotted with chalky barnacles that he picked at. His glasses dangled from his neck on a chain and had dandruff on the lenses. He held Bobby Popovic by the elbow and looked over at me and smiled but not nice. They spoke so that I could not hear them and he smiled at me again.

What you got there, Buster. Let me have a look, he said, and so I handed it to him all rolled up like I had it. He looked at it and squinted. Hmm, he said, putting eyes on me. That should be all right this time.

Bobby Popovic said, You crazy bastard, and he walked away mad.

Billy said he'd be right back and disappeared behind the shelves. He was humming Little Drummer Boy and I could only see part of his big white shirt so I took a Hershey's bar that would give me a cavity from a box on the counter and put it in the front of my pants. He came back around and handed me a paper bag and he fixed his glasses so that he was looking over the top of them at me. He smiled like before. His stare was milky, a pair of cat's-eye marbles. Tell her be careful and not too many at once, he said. He put a finger to his lips. Now shhhh, he said. You best not tell anybody, he said. He called me Buster again. This is the last time, he said.

She ate some right away in the car. Then at our room in the Hot L she told me I was her little man and she ate more medicine. She put all of them into her hand and she put all of them into her mouth.

That's better, she said. You're my little helper.

She washed them down with Cutty Sark from the green bottle with the yellow label and the pirate ship. She kept it in the bathtub. She put her head back. She drank some more and there was some on her chin in a white spot when she finished and I cleaned her up with a towel we'd stolen when we tried to live at the Howard Johnson's off the 91 rotary in Greenfield.

That's better, she said.

My mother rested her hand in my hair. She told me to put Fleetwood Mac on the record player. Then she was sleeping and I sat on the floor in the hall where the heat used to come through a vent. I ate the Hershey's bar that I stole from the drugstore. The act of chewing was hard and nutty and unfamiliar, and the heat wasn't coming through the vent because it never did anymore. She called out my name and then said something else. She did not open her eyes.

You were such my little helper, she said in a whisper. Little man. Medicine man.

Then she made an arcing motion with her arm like she was wiping away all the stars and from the dirty window overlooking the dead-end alley between the Hot L and the tannery the sky was a flat and empty black canvas but for a thumbprint smudge that had replaced the moon.

In the morning the record player was still going even though the music was finished. The needle ticked loudly like the second hand on a grandfather clock, only sporadic and full of static. Outside a northeast wind was a howling cold ghost that surrounded me. I closed my eyes against it and the sun and the glare from the snowbanks Joey Hostrop had sculpted from behind the wheel of his silver Ford F-250 all night long. And I told them from the payphone in front of Leo's TV on South Main that she was still sleeping. What kind of medicine, they said. I read it to them from the label on the little brown container and it took me three times to say it before I said it just right and they knew what it was. They asked me my name and said, Stay where you are.

WATCH OUT, TOWNIE BOY

Jabber has the limo. He picks me up at six and we get chocolate frappes from the pharmacy to throw at the fags in Northampton. I tell him about my mother and he laughs so hard he craps himself a little bit. He pulls over onto the shoulder. We're not downtown yet but there's a kid with blue hair at the bus stop. Jabber rolls up slow and I stick my head out the window as though to ask for directions and the kid with blue hair comes closer and I smash my chocolate frappe point blank on his face, the container and everything. It scares him and he's about to cry and Jabber guns the engine and we take off yelling all matter of redneck shit. I watch the kid getting smaller in my side mirror, cleaning up, probably actually crying now. Funny as hell to me, to us.

Fucking blue-haired faggot, Jabber says. He really has it in for the gays for some reason.

When we get by the church, he lets me drive so he can do one.

I see an older guy with tight jeans and a tight white alligator shirt with the collar flipped up and Jabber likes him right away for target practice. I stop at the red curb in front of a bar on Main Street called Fitzgerald's. Jabber whistles like he would at a cute girl and the guy comes over and Jabber gets him good. Standing still, the guy looks as though he's a melting statue at some wax museum, chocolate frappe dripping off his face in thin sheets. He starts hollering motherfucker this and motherfucker that, shaking his puny little fist, flipping us the bird.

We decide to hightail it since he's making a scene.

The last thing either one of us needs is another brush with the cops.

Then the guy is in the rearview mirror, standing bowlegged in the middle of the street, furious, a bunch of his gay buddies pouring out of the bar to find out what happened to him.

It's fucking hilarious.

Jabber laughs so hard he cries.

It's almost embarrassing.

I almost feel bad.

Fucking tight-jeans-wearing faggot, Jabber says.

Then he has to get the limo back to Griswald's Funeral Home because somebody died. He drops me at the Hot L, where I live upstairs in an apartment with my mother; she calls it a shit hole. She slings beers most evenings downstairs at the bar. But not tonight. Tonight she's in jail for stabbing her boyfriend in the neck with a busted Old Crow bottle. I smoke her cigarettes and watch television. There is a trail of blood from the kitchenette to the front door where I guess Tiny made his escape. He's over to Cooley Dick now. My mother barely missed an artery.

I call the hospital and he tells me he's okay, relatively speaking. All things considered, he says.

I laugh.

A cunt hair to the left and I'd be a goner, he says.

Jesus.

Your fucking mom, he says.

I agree in principle and we share a laugh. He's a good shit in my book. He's been dating my mom for three months and although we started off a little shaky we've become real chums. He sells cars over to Cherry's Used Auto in Ashfield and even promised to buy me a winter beater in November, when I'm old enough to drive. I don't know that he'll stay true especially if my mother gives him the oxygen, so I hope they can work things out at least until I turn sixteen and a half. He tells me they're going to release him in the morning and then he'll go to the bank and raise bail to get my mom out of Greenfield Correctional.

That's the kind of dude he is, that'll spring for a crazy broad after she cuts his jugular.

I sleep in my mother's bed and the next day Jabber hauls a group of preppy kids to the roller skating rink at the new shopping mall in Hadley and then we swing by Whitmore's for some beer. I have a fake ID. Richard Blake comes out from around back, where he lifts weights constantly. There's rumors he's on the juice and it wouldn't surprise me one bit. The guy is a fucking monster. His radio is blasting Bon Jovi singing "Dead or Alive." He grunts and nods his head, gets me a suitcase of Bud from the walk-in fridge. We drink and drive around Amherst and try to chase down some UMass pussy but those bitches are too stuck-up. Jabber almost went to college on a football scholarship but his knee blew out and he didn't have the grades. Mom tells me I should think about the Army for when I get out of high school but that's two years away.

Two years is like forever.

A lot can happen in two fucking years.

My mom tells me crazy skips a generation so I don't have anything to worry about. Out of the blue she says it, those are her exact words. Tiny spits whiskey through his nose and into his hand when he laughs at her statement, which feels to me like some sort of confession or apology.

Tiny has a big swath of gauze taped to the side of his neck, and he's given up trying to shave around it, he's given up trying to change the dressing daily. We're sitting at a high round table in the Bloody Brook Bar. All the regulars are in there at that hour. Everybody is teasing my mother and calling her Jackie the Ripper and she's taking it in stride, but Tiny turns red from embarrassment. I'm trying to bum a couple bucks off my mom so I can score some weed from Ty Mayfield. She's out of her tits so it won't be hard. I'm patient and listen to a drunken story or two. She goes to the shitter and Tiny digs in her purse, hands me a fistful of her tip money.

Don't spend it all in one place, he says. Like he's some kind of big shot all of a sudden. It's always easier to be generous with somebody else's dough, and I know he just wants to lose me so they can get romantic.

I meet Ty in the alley next to Rogers and Brooks and he sells me a dime bag. As I'm about to hand him the cash, Jabber sneaks up behind him and cracks him on top of the head with a length of pipe, making a sickening hollow sound at the point of contact.

What the fuck, I say.

That's exactly the kind of shit Jabber pulls sometimes. The kind of shit that'll come back to haunt us because Ty's older brother is a real old-school psycho, just out of Cedar Junction after a long stretch. Ty falls down unconscious and Jabber wants to hit him again but I make him stop so we don't do a fucking murder. That would be some really serious shit.

We just leave Ty there, a halo of black blood forming around his head.

Did you fucking hear that, Jabber says.

Back in the stretch limo Jabber is slamming his open hand on the dashboard trying to recreate the sound of the pipe hitting Ty's skull, which is impossible because it was so perfect when it happened. He's pretty amped up and so I roll a fat one quick to dial his adrenaline down; he can get out of control if I don't watch out. We stop in a cornfield to get high. Then there's a big bonfire at Hoosac's. We scoop up a couple townie skanks. Jabber whales on Mary Zablonski in the backseat while the Blow Job Queen earns her nickname up front with me.

Jabber calls Mary a whore once he's finished with her.

When he says whore he drags it out in a funny way so it rhymes with tour.

You're a dirty fucking whoooore, he says.

I laugh my ass off, he zips his pants, and she cries. The Blow Job Queen comes to her friend's defense but with a handle like that she doesn't have a leg to stand on. Then we take them to the BP Diner in Whately for biscuits and gravy. Mary pays the tab. She comes from money, her father owns the plastics factory. Her family thinks they're better than everybody. Then the Blow Job Queen puts quarters in the jukebox so I can listen to some Hank Junior. We dance around the place like assholes until Jimmy Duck emerges from the kitchen and tosses us out.

Fuck that guy, Jabber says outside.

Yeah, fuck the Duck, I say, trying to make him laugh.

The main problem with Jabber is he doesn't have an off switch.

We're standing in the parking lot. It rained some and there are puddles. The girls are shivering. I put my hands in my pockets. Jabber wants to go get the length of pipe from the trunk so he can teach Jimmy Duck a lesson too but I talk him down. It's not worth it, I say. He probably called the cops already, I say. We'll see him around town and he'll get what's coming. That kind of happy bullshit. People are watching us through the windows now. Jabber enjoys an audience. We pile into the limo and he squeals the tires and fishtails onto 5 and 10.

Fuck those motherfucking Polacks, Jabber says.

Mary smiles and sits right up against him like they're an old married couple.

Then I visit my mother over to the VFW. Tiny is there too, drinking brown booze for free and playing cards for coins with Robert Hawk Wilson and Boho. I eat a bowl of stale popcorn from the machine in the corner. Mom takes a cigarette break and sits down with me. She's been working double shifts to pay off all the fines related to the domestic battery charge. She takes her shoes off and rubs her yellow blistered feet. The ashes build up on the end of her Marlboro. My mother looks at me and doesn't say anything for a long time and that is never a good sign.

Hey, shit for brains, she finally says.

I try to think of what she might be pissed about.

Just like your old man, she says. That's supposed to be a hint but covers a lot of ground. I don't know what she's heard.

You think I'm not gone to hear about all the wrong things you do, she says.

I play dumb some more and stick a handful of that nasty popcorn in my mouth.

That's exactly how your father started and look where he ended up, she says, talking about prison, of course. After a few minutes she says, I'm sorry how things turned out, and sighs through a face full of smoke. How you turned out, she says. I did the best I could.

What a lie. My mother is a fucking liar. Lying to herself and to me. But I don't say anything. What the fuck I'm supposed to say to that. She means my father going away like he did. Me coming up without a role model, blah blah blah. All that silly nonsense. But I think I turned out just fine all things considered. I shrug and stare at the crumbs and burned kernels in my bowl. Lick the tip of my finger and dab at them, showing her that I'm bored out of my mind. Somebody at the bar calls her name and she tells him to fuck off and puts on her shoes. Stabs her cigarette into the overstuffed ashtray, asks me if I want any more popcorn.

Jabber does a couple three funerals. Then he takes some Northfield Mount Herman kids to Interskate 91. He tells me he gets to keep the limo overnight because he has to make a run to Bradley Airport wicked early in the morning. We hop onto 116. Jabber looks straight ahead and keeps his can of beer down when a statie pulls up along-side us at a red light. I keep mine down too. The fat fucking no-neck trooper eyeballing us, sizing us up for sure.

I smell bacon, I say.

Jabber laughs at a joke that never gets old.

The light turns green and the statie follows us close until around Bub's Bar-B-Q. Then he accelerates with blue gumballs flashing and is long gone in a matter of seconds.

We play a couple hands of poker with Richard Wickline and Chris Powers in the booth at the pharmacy. Alice brings us straw-berry frappes and a bowl of French fries. Jabber wins two dollars and we leave it on the table and go next door to the packy. Big Ben sneaks us a twelver of tall boys out the back. He calls us the Future Fuckups of America. Jabber tells him to kiss our hairy asses. Then there are a couple nip-size bottles of Jack Daniel's in the console bar in the white stretch. We drink those too. Jabber puts the AC on full blast and drives down Long Plain Road, on to Whately Road parallel to the Connecticut River that stinks and then he pulls off into some of Walter Sadoski's corn that must be nine feet tall.

We listen to Def Leppard singing "Pour Some Sugar on Me" and pound some beers.

Jabber takes two more out of the cooler. These fuckers are going down good, he says. We sit there with the windows up and the engine idling, the AC, the loud music. What should we do now, Jabber says in between songs, then he gives me his goofy look that always makes me nervous.

I tell him let's ride into Hamp so we can make fun of the hippies and the homos.

That snaps him out of it. All right, he says. He slaps the steering wheel with his open hand. What the fuck, he says. It's something to do. Better than working for a living. He hits me on the arm and his knuckles are hard and flat from punching the heavy bag he keeps chained to a crossbeam in his father's garage. When he can't sleep at night he'll jump rope and smack that thing for hours.

Jabber revs the engine and follows FarmAll tractor tracks past row after row of corn. The river is a blue gash that keeps Stillwater from spilling down Sunsick Mountain and into the center of Bucktown. A couple busloads of Puerto Ricans from Holyoke and West Springfield are picking strawberries at Nourse Farms for $2.50 an hour. They wear white T-shirts wrapped around their heads or hanging from the backs of their pants. A few of them look at us and cough at the dirt the limo kicks up. They'll wander into town on payday and we'll have to fuck them up for taking away our summer jobs. Last year Jabber made two hundred bucks a week picking tobacco, it pisses him off just thinking about it. Fucking spics, he says. Then the back tires screech onto the blacktop and round brown flies spread their kamikaze guts on the windshield.

Rich kids from New York and California come to Franklin County every autumn for the fancy schools. Millionaire parents wanting their babies safe and away from the dangers of big cities. That's all fine and good, but it's clear they look down their noses at people like us.

People who live here by default.

We're not real to them. We don't seem to matter much. As though we're fucking invisible.

A couple girls are smoking cigarettes, sitting in the grass in front of the used record store.

I can tell they're not local. I can always tell.

We pull up against the curb.

Hey there, ladies, Jabber says.

They look at us and each other and giggle. Jabber tells them to come for a ride. So just like that they climb in back and the pretty one asks right off what we have for them to drink.

Jabber laughs and shifts into drive.

Then the pretty one looks at me. How come you get this fancy car with a driver, she says.

What a fucking retard.

You somebody famous, she says.

I tell her I'm going to be famous someday. I tell her my daddy set up a trust fund. I tell her Jabber is my bodyguard and he knows karate and he has a black belt and always packs heat. I tell her I'm at UMass studying to be an astronaut—just taking up space. Jabber laughs and adjusts the rearview mirror and the girls look at each other and giggle some more. They know I'm full of shit but they play along. It's make-believe time. They know we'll say anything to get into their panties and we know they're slumming and everybody wants the same thing in the end.

Jabber buys a couple four-packs of wine coolers at Watroba's. The pretty one rides shotgun and I stay in back with the other one who looks better up close. She smells nice too. She doesn't

smell like any girl I've ever known. I tell her so and she says I'm
sweet. Her name is Abby and they're freshmen at Smith College.
It's starting to get dark and Jabber drives to the maze, a network
of tall hedges with dead ends and turnarounds. It's a well-known
make-out spot. We park the car. I know the course by heart but
don't admit it and Abby holds my leather belt so I don't lose her.
We get to the middle and she lets me kiss her and she tastes like
cherry-flavor Lifesavers. We sit under the orange moon and touch
each other outside our clothes a little bit and she asks me if I really
go to UMass. I confess that I'm not even old enough yet and she
tells me I sure seem old enough. I ask what she means by that and
she says I have an old spirit.

She says it with a certain amount of reverence.

She says some people get old before their time because of what
they experience at an early age. It could be anger or pain or frustra-
tion. The deep feeling that they have been wronged in some horrible
fashion. It could be that they truly were abused or neglected when
they were children, in a vulnerable state. So what happens is they
basically skip past their childhood. She calls these people Old Souls.
It sounds like she's reciting something you can learn in a book. It
sounds clinical.

She doesn't know what the fuck she's talking about. Not really.
Not yet.

I tell her maybe that's true about what happens. And that if it
doesn't fucking kill you, well, you know the rest.

She giggles but not the same as before. She senses that something has suddenly changed in me. That I can't swallow my anger
down like a bitter pill any longer.

Her pretty friend calls out but I know Jabber will keep her busy
and they won't interrupt me. Fat black crickets chirp like sentries
protecting us. Then she grabs onto my wrist when I'm messing with

the small white buttons of her blouse and she tells me that I have all that oldness but also the impatient hands of a high school boy. Abby or whatever her real name is wants to keep on talking but I'm all done talking. I hold her arms together behind her head with my left hand. She says she doesn't want to do it, but that's a fucking lie. And I'm tired of all the lies.

DAMN THE WIND

Gramps said it was a hurricane. We used candles that were in pickle jars and almost smelled like purple grapes. We used a transistor radio, and the ocean was loud and white and came into the yard of the house on Raymond Street. The wind was a rowdy bully too. It whooped and knocked down trees and telephone wires and pushed white sailboats onto their sides in Kettle Cove, smashed them on the rocks along the beach in front of the Bath and Tennis Club where the rich kids went. Gramps let me take a flashlight to bed because my owl nightlight didn't work from the storm. He told me the flashlight was for emergencies, and he told me my mother had a screw loose. That's why they've got her locked up, he said. They should throw away the fucking key, he said. You shouldn't listen to any of her nonsense, he said.

I listened to the wind, and the unbreakable rain that was popcorn on my window. To the ocean that sounded like gunfire. I didn't sleep for fear of it and all the rest. Gramps didn't sleep either for his own private reasons and in the morning his eyeballs were maraschino cherries floating in grenadine and he used an iron garden rake to knock wires off the roof. The alcoholic watched from the porch. She always watched everything. She wore a blue raincoat and a blue rain hat. She had a whiskey bitter in her good hand. Be careful, she said.

Careful careful careful. He ignored her and slapped at the wires that were fat and patient snakes.

Gramps didn't talk to the alcoholic because he was mad about the wind and the rain and the ocean coming into the yard. He was mad about the maple trees that were sideways in front of the house. The trees are dead, he said. God and the trees are dead. I had on a rubber coat and the alcoholic buttoned it up to my neck. The wind pushed sand and rain against me and I could hear the sharp shards of them on my coat and feel them on my face and legs like a million bee stings. I waved at the alcoholic up on the porch and she waved her drink at me. She had her free hand on the collar of her blue raincoat and she shrugged and shivered. Then she watched Gramps. She took a drink. Before the stroke in the basement that Gramps called a stroke of bad luck, she liked to say she loved me to death. Now all she could muster was Love love love.

Gramps was big and wet. He finally got the wires off the roof. Watch out, he said. For Christ sakes watch out, he told me. He put the garden rake in the shed where he kept the riding lawn mower and his tools. I followed him around but he didn't talk to me because he cursed at the wind and the rain. Goddamn the wind, he said. Goddamn rain. Your mother is filling everybody's head with shit, he said. I never touched her. Not like that, he said. You believe me, don't you.

The ocean was not white anymore. It was not in the yard anymore. Pieces of sailboats were everywhere. Lobster traps were busted, misshapen. Neighbors in ponchos and teenagers with surfboards stood on the cement wall like curious birds and looked up at the sky that was a black bruise from the flat part of an open hand. Waves ominous and rolling. Seagulls floated on chunks of wood and old unhitched buoys with identification numbers burned onto them.

Gramps smelled like gasoline and skunk cabbage and he cut the trees in the yard with a chainsaw from the shed. He wore glasses to keep the yellow dust out of his eyes. He wore waxy plugs to keep the noise out of his ears. There was a cigarette stuck in his face where his mouth was so thin it looked like it was nothing but a tear in his flesh. I followed him. I put my fingers in my ears and slammed my eyes shut. He told me to get back. For Christ sakes get back, he said. You're just like your goddamn mother. She never heeded me either.

The chainsaw was a screaming yellow devil in his hands. The alcoholic was on the porch with the tripod telescope to look at the tugboats and the tankers going into port. Careful, she said. Careful careful careful. Gramps didn't pay her any mind and he cut the trees with the chainsaw and I put my fingers in my ears. The alcoholic put her fingers in her ears too and she placed her drink on the railing to do it. Then she finished it and shrunk specter-like into the dark doorway.

After dinner the lights worked and the television worked and Gramps said the hurricane went up the coast. He said that the other cape would get hit pretty hard too. Come over here, boy, he said. He wasn't mad anymore and I sat in his lap. He let me hold his tall can of beer and it was cold. He drank it from a mug he ran under the tap and stored in the icebox. The alcoholic looked outside toward Lexington Avenue and the beauty parlor and made a clicking noise with her tongue and said, Storm storm storm. Then they fell asleep in their chairs with the television.

My nightlight that was an owl worked again too. It was orange and it had black eyes and it leered with a black clown mouth. I got under my blanket where it was dark and warm and maybe safe but there was some sand from the storm on my sheets and it scratched me. Then Gramps came into my room because I heard him on the floor. And the hinges of the door squeaked like the significant sobs of summer crickets that crunched like nuts when you walked on them. Don't be afraid now, boy, Gramps said. It's nothing but a little squall, he said. Then he shuddered like a busted Coke machine and put his fat face in mine and it was so red I thought it was going to pop.

MAIN STREET INCIDENT

Fog fell like a dead dog on Jonesy. He was standing in front of the Hot L waiting for anybody to sneak him in so he could shoot some stick. I tapped my horn and he looked up and then got into my 1967 Mustang. We parked in the alley between the twenty-four-hour coin-operated laundry and Boron's Market and drank a couple long-neck Budweiser beers I had on ice in a five-gallon pail in the backseat. He showed me how his hands and forearms and neck were brown and sticky from picking tobacco all day down to Smiaroski's farm. He said it was nigger work and that old man Smiaroski was a senile prick. Then we scrapped with a couple yahoos who came out of the bar shoving each other around and across Main Street, right into my brand-new paint job. Candy-apple red. I only broke an empty bottle on the one and he took off running, but Jonesy really snapped and knocked the other dude's teeth out against the cement curb.

Can you believe that shit, I said.

Fucking redneck motherfuckers.

We left and took the back roads to Hatfield before Westy and LaPinta got the call and came by in the black-and-white. Jonesy had some killer green that he grew on the edge of his father's property up north. He rolled up a fat one to the light of my stereo. His hands were teeth-cut and still shaking I guess from thumping on the guy

out in the street, but he did all right with the joint. He was a year behind me but didn't go to school anymore because of his temper. I was
going to be a junior at Franklin County Tech in the fall. My mother
wanted me to learn a trade and amount to something, but she wasn't
going to hold her breath. We stopped about a half mile up the dirt
road to the reservoir and smoked with the windows all the way open
to the smell of the corn harvest and the rest of Johnny Baronas' farm.
Jonesy told me a judge in Greenfield was making him live with his
grandmother but he mostly slept in abandoned barns.

A mob of black bats passed before us like windblown leaves.
Then we drove around some more and parked in the same spot
across from the Hot L. Jonesy called it the scene of the crime. The
music inside was loud but hard to figure out from where we were
because of all the sloppy people talking and laughing and because
of the August heat too. It sounded like ZZ Top. Jonesy said if he
could just get one lousy game that would make his night. I told him
maybe on a Wednesday or something but they were really cracking
down on weekends. Kim Streeter from my driver's ed class came
out of the coin-op with some other girl. They were drinking wine
coolers and they got in the car with us and I moved it back a bit to
get out of the streetlight.

Kim asked me about my girlfriend, Beth, and the rumors she
heard. Then I mugged on her in the front seat for a while and she was
wearing one of those front-snap bras I liked. Her nipples were pink
and hard like the unused erasers on a couple number-two pencils. I
let Kim give me head while Jonesy got the other girl high. I adjusted
the mirror so he could watch. Then he tried to kiss his girl and his
sticky hand got stuck in her hair and she freaked out and he hit her
and kept hitting her with his fist like she was a dude until I dragged
her out of the car and told her and Kim to go away. Her nose looked
broke. I said, Jesus, and Jonesy sat in front with me and finished his

beer then got out without saying anything and walked right into the bar. I waited fifteen minutes and when there was no sign of any trouble I figured everything was all right.

I crossed the Bucktown Bridge and took River Road to see Beth. I parked in a small clearing in the wooded area on Hollabird's property so her parents wouldn't wake up. She let me in through a window and told me about her cousin Myra taking her down to the clinic in Springfield. She had to go twice because we waited so long. They had to put tubes in me, she said. I didn't want anybody touching her like that but she was strong about it. I told her I was sorry and she said it was her fault too. I told her about Jonesy acting up and she said I had a responsibility to keep him straight. She said it made her nervous how he was always trying to impress me and I'd better be careful. Whatever, I said. I asked her if they had to cut her at all.

No, she said. They just had to stretch me and put tubes in there.

That's good then, I said.

Then I watched television and she cried until she fell asleep.

Westy and LaPinta came to see me when I was starting my shift in the morning. I told Geno I was going to use his phone to get the specs on a water pump and I took them into the office and sat on a stack of used snow tires. They said that somebody saw my car out in front of the Hot L. They said there was some big trouble down there and did I see anything. They said Jonesy finally crossed the wrong person and got his block knocked off with a two-by-four. He was in a coma down to Cooley Dick. It didn't look good. I told them a pack of lies about my whereabouts and they knew it but were too lazy to follow up. They were just part-time cops.

Jonesy died a week later and his grandma hired a lawyer from Hartford to sue the Hot L for letting him go in there in the first place.

She called me on the phone to say that if I showed up for the funeral her nephews from Colrain would feed me into a wood chipper. In the paper they said he had dope and booze in him but other stuff too. The kind of stuff I could buy on a corner in Holyoke. The bartender at the Hot L said he didn't serve Jonesy a single drink that night.

I saw Kim around town and she never mentioned it. I saw that other girl sometimes and her nose was crooked for a while but then she must have paid to get it fixed. Beth told me I was poison. She told me I was like a cancer that contaminated anybody who got close. She told me I could have stopped him but that I enjoyed exposing the rot in others. She said I didn't recognize the influence I had over people. She blamed Jonesy and everything on me. She didn't want to be my girlfriend anymore. What the fuck, I said. Her old man held a shotgun on me and told me to stop coming around and so that's exactly what I did.

LISTEN TO THAT
TRAIN WHISTLE BLOW

We smoke dope in the graveyard next to the stone marked Harry Arms. There's a cricket that sounds like a busted box spring. Shelly isn't wearing a bra and we bump against each other and when I finish I tell her about the train and she cries. At first she doesn't want me to leave. Then she wants to come with me. If I were old enough to legally drive a car, she could come. But hopping trains is not the kind of business a girl should get involved with. That's how I explain it. She cries some more. It seems like she's always crying about one thing or another. She scratches my name into her arm with a beer bottle cap where everybody can see. Stupid fucking bitch.

An early autumn breeze that smells like cow shit.

Get dressed, I say.

I thought I'd be your girl forever, she says.

Forever is a long fucking time, Shell.

My old man gets drunk at the Bloody Brook Bar and locks me out of the apartment on purpose so I hotwire his F-250 and drive it into the tri-town pond. Let him find it like that. I walk across Don Milewski's empty pumpkin patch. The side door of Boron's Market on Eastern Avenue is easy to jimmy and I need supplies for my train ride. I stuff a plastic trash bag with cupcakes, beef jerky, and chocolate milk. A flashlight and batteries. A pouch of Red Man chewing tobacco. There's a dusty old cat with only one eyeball living in the back and he meows at me.

He hisses and spits, and I laugh at him.

You're only a cat and that's all you'll ever be.

I want to go to California but I don't even know what that means. I hide in a bush by the tracks. It will slow down to make the bend past Dry Run Bridge. If I've seen it once, I've seen it a million times. Raping Ray is drinking coffee in a Styrofoam cup. I don't notice him at first. He walks quiet like an Indian. Nobody knows for sure if he did it or not and besides it was a long time ago and he's harmless now. I'm not scared of him. He asks me what I'm doing. I tell him my plan.

He says that it's the Boston and Maine line so I can only go north or south. Forget California, he says. Maybe the French part of Canada.

That's okay by me.

A mosquito bites him on the neck and he slaps it against his skin and leaves a smudge.

He sits on a stump. How's your father, he says because they're the same age, came up together.

I hope he gets hit by a truck, I tell him.

Raping Ray laughs hard and spills some coffee that stains his pant leg.

The train never comes. Motherfucker this and motherfucker that. My old man smacks me about the F-250 and more when I deny it. He passes out on the couch and I put his cigarettes in the toilet that doesn't work and has not been flushed in days. Shelly meets me at the Bucktown Creamy. She's happy that I didn't leave and she cries. We share a large vanilla cone. Then I steal somebody's two-tone Gran

Torino to drive up Mount Toby. A giant tree casts a long shadow on a faded red barn. The letters of my name are scabs on her pale flesh. We get in the backseat and she begs me to leave it inside her and so I do. When I'm done it sounds like a cow pulling its foot out of the mud. She smiles white teeth. Van Halen is on the radio singing, I got it bad.

If I have your baby then you got to stay, she says.

If you do then I'll throw it in the river.

She cries.

My shift pumping gas starts at five. Eugene tells me that LaPinta wants to ask me about a certain F-250 in a certain pond. I guess my old man called the cops. They towed it out and wanted to throw the book at him because there is already a stack of DWIs. Later in the evening, Janet from the pharmacy brings me a cheeseburger and fries for dinner. It's one of the perks. There's a busted button on her overalls and I can see a bit of her red nylon panties. I tell her about the train too. We both get off at eight and so she comes by with strawberry frappes and I know exactly where Killer Kowalski hides a bottle of rotgut in his red rollaway toolbox. I shut down the pumps and lock the doors, and we sit in the office and drink clear booze and then I let her jerk me off. Then she sticks her gum behind her ear and bobs on me with piston-like efficiency. I don't consider it cheating, but Shelly might have a whole different opinion on the matter.

School is a joke. I get high with Shell out by the Dwire Lot during third-period English. Bobcat and Rosey are there too. We burn a fat one and laugh and listen to a bunch of brown-noser kids playing tennis during physical education. Viola Goodnow is yelling instructions and Bob is impersonating her dead on. Fucking hilarious. And then instead of going back to class with all the losers we hitchhike to Red Rock. We don't get a ride and it's a long walk down 116 and I tell

Bobcat and Rosey about the train. Shelly cries when I say I'm leaving her behind.

Jesus fucking Christ, I say, it's for your own good.

Bobcat's mom strips at the Shed. He doesn't like to talk about it. We steal some Swisher Sweets from my old man, who is in a booze coma as usual. The Red Sox are on the tube. We go into the hall and climb out the window and onto the roof and the moon looks like a banana. Bob has a half pint of blackberry brandy that he lifted from the packy. He takes a tug and gives it to me. Across the street there are some Puerto Ricans getting beat up in front of the Brook. Murph and a couple other guys from Double D's are really pissed about something and smashing bottles all over the spics. By the time Westy and LaPinta show up with the flashing lights everybody is gone and there is just a lot of broken glass and blood and somebody's torn shirt on the sidewalk. They look around and talk to Fydo, who owns the place. Then the game ends because my old man turns the volume down. Bobcat blows smoke rings.

This place sucks, he says, meaning the Hot L roof, the town, the whole valley.

We stay quiet for a few beats to let his statement sink in.

Yeah, I say, I'm a hop that fucking train tomorrow, boy.

It feels good to say it aloud, but Bobcat doesn't say anything back and he doesn't even look at me. Fuck him. I know he thinks I'll never do it. I spit over my shoulder and it lands on the ledge. The problem is that I already talked it to death. The idea. The concept of getting away. That's what happens sometimes when you put things into words: you kill them.

There is the smell of pickles from Oxford. I take my old man's F-250 just back from the shop and drive it into the tri-town pond again. Janet is already there and we skinny dip. She asks me about the pickup and I tell her I'm testing it for leaks. She laughs. The water is warm and the harvest moon is reflected in it. She tells me about her shift at the BP Diner. She's trying to save money for college. We swim to the middle and sit on the floating dock. I kiss her and she tastes like deep-fried onion rings. Then we swim to the rope swing and take turns diving and flipping. She's athletic for a girl and can do almost everything I can do. We end up back on the beach. There's some weed that I bought from Skid Syska and we torch a doobie under the white lifeguard chair. She asks me about the train. She says she can totally picture me hanging out in California, and then she uses her mouth on me again. Afterward she just sits there and I skip a flat rock on the pond's smooth black surface.

I hear Shelly went to the clinic, she says, her eyes wide-set like a plastic doll's.

I look at her and then away. You hear loads of stupid shit if you listen long enough, I tell her.

Chuck Smiaroski says he's going to dock my pay for being late. I tell him a lie, that my old man crashed the F-250 again and I had to walk to the farm, but Chuck doesn't care because he's a redneck asshole. I cut field tobacco until noon and then Bobcat comes to get me. He tells me Chuck has been bitching all morning and wants to shit can me.

We use pitchforks to load up brown heads of cabbage that they can use for relish at Oxford. The sun is crazy hot and I take my T-shirt off and put it in my back pocket. Bob has a water jug in the Chevy and he gets it for me. We stand there for a minute. There are bugs flying into my ears and eyes and nose and I shoo them away. Chuck pays cash on Fridays and he makes a big point of holding some of mine back. He tells me I need an attitude adjustment.

I tell him to fuck off.

I tell him about the train.

See, I don't need your dumbass nigger job, I say.

Oh yah hey, I used to have big dreams too, kid. He laughs when he says it.

He adjusts his balls and laughs and spits over his shoulder and gives us a six-pack of Budweiser and tells us not to drink it all in one place. Bobcat has his mom's T-bird and we drive around listening to Billy Squire until he has to get it back so she can get to the Shed on time. He says that Philo Reno gave his mom a black eye last time she was late. He drops me at the common exactly when there's a train running north. Bob waves and pulls away and I stand in the middle of the street. Brake lights and he waits at the crossing. Puffs of white smoke rise like seven little ghosts escaping from the tailpipe. I count and watch them disappear. Sense that he's watching me in the rear-view. That he expects me to do something. Anything. But I'm frozen. Then the train is too fast and loud and it shakes everything in town, even me. And then the red-and-white-painted arms go up and the orange light stops flashing and Bobcat drives off real slow.

I hit her and it feels good. Shelly cries, of course, and I say there's a first time for everything. My old man laughs until he spits blood when I tell him she's knocked up.

Holy shit, boy—*cough*—you done did her this time—*cough cough cough spit.*

He reminds me that I was an accident too.

That's always been very clear to me.

Shelly's too far along to get it taken care of proper and so her parents kick her out of the house when she starts to show. I tell her it's prob-ably not even mine and she gets sick on my brand-new Dunham steel-toe boots. She goes to live with her aunt with the horse farm in Shelburne Falls.

Bobcat can't believe my bad luck. We get shitfaced and drive around town and up past the river and over Stillwater Bridge and down Old Hoosac's Road. He parks in the corn for a minute so we can piss and he gets his brother's shotgun from the trunk and we sit back in the car and then we shoot out some streetlights and put four holes in the stop sign at 116 and Sawmill Plain. Then there's a party on Bull Hill and we stand around the bonfire that smells like burning tires. Janet is there with her new boyfriend from the Shutesbury AC. She gives me a sideways look because I never called her like I promised I would. But what the fuck, I never call anybody. Bobcat laughs and I laugh too, even though I don't mean it as much as he does.

How was your big train ride, she says loud, like trying to get my goat.

All eyes are on me now.

Richard here says he's going to California, Janet says.

That's when Shutesbury really sizes me up, a wad of chew under his bottom lip. He lets go a stream of brown saliva that hits the dirt. That boy right there ain't going nowheres, he says.

You can hear a pin drop for a few heartbeats, then everybody laughs as though I'm the biggest joke in town. Bobcat slaps me on the back. Minutes pass like one of Max Ante's eighteen-wheelers. Black smoke all around makes it hard to breathe. Whosever bright idea it was to burn Eagle GTs. People start to leave. You can hear engines turning and car radios cooing Bryan Adams and Janet is sitting right up against her new boyfriend in his shiny new GMC and they are trying to pass, if I'd just get out of the way. Vehicles line up behind him and he shines his brights on me and punches his horn and I just stand there and close my eyes. Bobcat is trying to say something but I can barely hear him. Shelly called from a payphone the other night to tell me it's a boy and she's going to name him after me, which is some fucked-up shit. As far as I'm concerned, my name is just a series of little white scars on her arm.

Somewhere behind me a train whistle blows, long and low. A farm dog answers the train and then a second dog joins in. They sing out like that for a long time. And when their voices fade away and I open my eyes I'm all alone, and it's quiet as a dream.

SOMETIMES THERE'S GOD

The old man has a stroke some weeks after Harlan Bovet's mother goes missing. Harlan hates his father even more now that he's a fucking invalid. The emotion was already there, but deep and buried, and now it has bubbled to the surface. He visits because it's a pleasure to watch him die. There's a Puerto Rican girlfriend from the old man's past who is nice enough and cleans him up when he shits his pants, which is all the time, as far as Harlan can tell. Her name is Lila. She waits tables at the Howard Johnson's by the Greenfield rotary, and she suddenly reappeared when Harlan's mother vanished. She wheels the old man around the house with his oxygen tanks and takes over Harlan's old bedroom. There's a stray cat living in the room next to the garage where Harlan crashes sometimes when Annabelle throws him out. His old man doesn't recognize Harlan. Lila uses a paper towel to wipe spittle from his chin.

How is he, Harlan says.

Good days and bad days.

All right.

Mostly like this, she says.

I don't know how you do it.

Some days I don't either.

I hear how he talks to you.

Yeah, and that's on the good days.

Harlan laughs. Lila is all right in his book. She gets him a can of Budweiser beer and she has a highball with a green olive stuck through with a toothpick. The old man simply stares out the window at the haze and into the pitch of night and drools some more.

He doesn't even know me anymore, Harlan says.

No, he does.

Not that I'm complaining.

It just takes time to register.

If he knew it was me drinking his beer he'd be pissed, Harlan says.

Lila laughs. She asks him about Annabelle.

Oh, she's still around, he says.

And have you heard from your mother then.

Nah, he says. She's probably down to Florida.

Well, I cleaned up that room in case you need it.

Much obliged.

Clean sheets and everything.

All right.

The works.

Thanks.

Just in case. You still have your key.

Sure, he says. I have it somewhere.

Well, don't be a stranger.

I know.

He's your father, after all.

Don't remind me.

It's Lila's turn to laugh.

Harlan gives her a hug and she takes the empty can from him and disappears into the kitchen so he can have a moment with his father. A gurgle in the old man's throat. Harlan moves close so they're face to face and he looks for a trace of the mean old bastard he remembers but all that's left is a pathetic and empty human shell. He uses the back of his own sleeve to wipe white bile from his father's dry prune lips. Harlan is greased and feels one of his episodes coming on and so he naps in the chair for a couple hours. It feels good to be so completely alone.

He rides to the Ashfield Lake House and orders a Jack and Coke. There isn't much going on. He drinks three more and then takes his bike back down Route 116 and through the center of town. He sees the woman in front of the Hot L, Nikki from the other night, who hired him to drill the dude at Joey D's. He pulls over and removes his helmet, and at first she doesn't recognize him. Then she smiles, drags on her cigarette, plays it cool like.

What you doing, he says.

I don't know.

Well, he says. Hop the fuck on. He gives her his extra helmet and she hops on, flicking her cigarette into the street. Annabelle is in the back of his mind. Where to, he says.

Wherever.

They go down the mountain and cross the river to Mike's Westview. Harlan puts the bike out back beside a pile of lumber. They go inside and lean against the high bar, order some drinks.

So the other night, she says.

Yeah.

That's what you do.

What's that now.

The thing you did for me.

What about it.

Well, she says. Is that what you do.

I do it sometimes.

You give out beatings for a living.

That wasn't a beating.

What do you call it then.

I don't call it nothing.

Nikki laughs and sips her drink and looks at Harlan.

Anyhow, she says. He's up to his old tricks again.

That same guy, you mean. Did he hit you.

Worse than that, he kicked me out.

You're saying that's worse than getting hit.

In a college town it is, she says. You try to find an apartment in September.

But you really thought he'd let you stay after that.

I don't know.

After I said your name so he knew it was you sent me.

I guess I didn't know.

Right.

Or think it through.

Harlan looks at her.

He used to love me, she says after a minute.

I bet.

Maybe it was a test.

So.

Yeah exactly, she says. So fucking what.

Nikki finishes her cheap version of a cosmopolitan and they go to Harlan's parents' garage and sit in the spare room and smoke a joint. He's drunk enough he tells her all about Annabelle and describes her as the love of his life, but Nikki doesn't give a shit about that. They kiss and she uses her hand on him and then she stands up and takes her clothes off. He watches. Then he stands up and gets undressed too and she turns around and grabs the kitchenette sink and puts him deep inside her. They bump against each other like that for a while.

Then, lying on the mattress to catch their breaths, they hear Harlan's father upstairs cursing. It sounds like he's throwing things and flipping furniture over and Harlan laughs. He tells her about his old man, the history there. He calls her Darling Nikki after the song by Prince.

So he's just dying up there, she says.

Dying or already dead.

Sounds like he's got some life left in him.

Maybe hate keeps him going.

Hate.

He had enough of that, I seem to recall, Harlan says.

Darling Nikki puts her head on his chest. So what do we do now.

Just lay here for a minute and rest and be real fucking quiet.

He puts his finger to his lips. Shhhhhhh, he says.

I mean after that, she says.

After that you'll do what you do, he says. And I'll do what I do.

Darling Nikki likes the way that sounds, prefers being the other woman. Later she tells him she's crashing at a friend's house in Whately so that's where he drops her. He doesn't mind at all. There is a little dog barking out front and she calls him Bushy. He's a Jack Terrier. She tells Harlan that Bushy caught a squirrel the other day and whipped it around like they do and broke its neck. Then she doesn't know if she should kiss him goodbye or hug him or maybe nothing at all, so she just stands there and he rides off without saying anything.

Annabelle takes Harlan up north to clear his head. She says the fresh air will do him good. They climb Mount Watroba and sleep in a tent. They find a gentle bend in a river where they can swim naked and nobody else is around. Everywhere else there are busloads of people. She isn't much for roughing it, so it's good they have access to bathrooms

with running water and big metal lock boxes that are bear-proof.
The second night they eat pizza in some one-horse town and Harlan
drinks three pitchers of beer until they won't sell him anymore and
close the window on him. It's mostly college students working there
and they don't know what to make of the man with the scars and the
cauliflower ears and the beautiful young woman.

This must be a great job, Harlan says. For somebody in their
twenties.

Walking back to their tent to go to sleep, there are puddles from
a storm that had just missed them. Harlan splashes Annabelle to try
to make her laugh but she isn't having any of it. Harlan splashes and
splashes until some random guy tells him he got his wife wet. Harlan
puts on doll eyes and tells the dude to fuck off. Annabelle sees where
it's going so she wraps him up and practically drags him away.

He could've asked nice but he was doing that for his wife, he
says. Showing her how big and brave he is in his L.L. Bean camping
outfit right out of the catalogue. Then Harlan lets Annabelle think
she saved him even though the truth of the matter is he was just too
lazy to whip the guy's butt at that particular moment.

She tells him she was embarrassed and she won't let up on him.
Then Harlan sings to her, trying to be funny, and eventually gets
impatient and somewhat rough. He's still feeling playful so he makes
wolf or coyote sounds until she shushes him and people in the nearby
tents ask him to shut the Christ up.

Harlan closes his eyes.

When he opens them Annabelle tells him he ruined everything.
It's morning now. He doesn't remember, which is a result of the booze
and the drugs and all those years of fighting. She tells him she cried all
night long and that his snoring was worse than ever. He feels like shit
about it, and he sits on a set of wooden steps and smokes and campers
are giving him looks, but of course nobody dares say anything.

They walk in a meadow and there's too much sun for Harlan so he sits on a dead tree in the shade until she wakes him, tells him that he's killing himself and Harlan thinks maybe she's right. She wants him to quit scrapping and he wants her to quit stripping but then what would they do. Back on the bike he feels better, like an old-time cowboy in that setting and with her holding on tightly to him, her warm breath on the back of his neck when they stop to look at a pair of deer that are lost. It's a deep-chested buck and a white-nosed doe and in a rare moment of reflection Harlan says, Look, it's me and you. Annabelle laughs and that's the first sign of something good in a long while.

Kerosene Dream is playing at the Seven O's. Annabelle is wearing a short skirt for the occasion, and at intermission Bart D'Armand sits with them backstage and they smoke a joint and talk about back in the day, bareknuckling at the scrapyard. Bart was tough back then but lacked killer instinct and that was before he started the band. Then Bart has to finish his set but Harlan and Annabelle stay behind, sitting on a speaker case. They can hear the music, Bart singing about his old Country Squire. Harlan gets on his knees and uses his mouth on her.

Afterward it takes Annabelle a few minutes to catch her breath.

Oh my God, she finally says.

Don't drag him into this.

I need a cigarette.

Harlan lights two and hands one to Annabelle.

I don't know how you do that, she says through a smoke ring.

Harlan laughs.

I'm serious, she says. That's something else, boy.

Harlan laughs again and holds her hand and they walk back out into the bar area and order a couple more drinks. He can still taste her, ripe cantaloupe. Then it's her third drink and that puts her past her limit lately and she's fading fast. After Bart does his last song, Harlan takes her home. She isn't keen on the idea of him staying out without her but she's too tired to argue, so she makes him promise to keep it in his pants.

Harlan meets Tim Looney at the Filling Station. They eat cheeseburgers and French fries and drink chocolate frappes.

Tim clears his throat. So listen, he says. Here's the thing.

Tim tells Harlan about the trouble with his asshole brother trying to scam his elderly parents out of their house in Bucktown, and now maybe even trying to poison them to get his filthy mitts on his inheritance. How there's no talking to the guy and Tim is at his wit's end.

Harlan looks at him when he's done talking.

I need some help, Tim speaks up. And I heard some shit about what you do.

Well, I don't know what you heard.

That maybe you could talk to him.

You just said there's no talking.

I don't know what else to do, Tim says. Where else to go.

Just get it straight what you want to happen besides talking and let me know.

Tim covers dinner and Harlan shakes his hand and unfurls his plastic poncho. It's raining, coming at him sideways. Harlan considers waiting it out but he doesn't know how long that will be.

He calls Sonny from the payphone in the diner.

Yeah.

Sonny.

Where you at, Sonny says.

Just ate at the Station.

Hey, somebody here wants to say hello.

There's a woman's voice. Harlan doesn't recognize her at first. She's teasing him, calling him the Boogie Man, Franklin County Badass, Southpaw. He plays along until he figures it out. It's Sherry. Her twin Mary is in the background, wrestling around with Sonny, it sounds like.

Well, shit, he says.

Harlan could use some company, a drink.

Come over and see us, Sherry says. Why don't you.

You read my mind. See you soon.

The wind tilts the Harley and makes it hard to handle on the slick blacktop so Harlan takes it slow to Sonny's one-room shithole on Main Street in Turners Falls, right above Waters and Sons Plumbing. Mary is sitting on Sonny's lap and Sherry is mixing up a cocktail.

Look what the cat dragged in, Sonny says.

He has coke in his new handlebar mustache that he calls the Firefighter Special.

Hey, Harlan says.

You're soaked, Sherry says.

Yeah, it's coming down good now.

Sherry hands him a drink and he takes a long tug off of it.

Ahhhhh.

Well, let's get you out of those wet clothes, she says. Before you catch your death.

She takes his hand and leads him to the small bedroom in back. Sonny laughs and Mary does too. Harlan can hear them chopping up some more blow. Sherry undresses Harlan and then she gets undressed too so they can take a hot shower together. The water on his skin hurts at first. She looks good with her black hair wet. He grabs it like a ponytail behind her head and pulls back and uses his mouth on her neck and tits. Then he picks her up and carries her to Sonny's bed, which smells like fast food, and eventually they end up sweaty and sticking to each other with whatever didn't end up inside her.

Harlan gets a headache and closes his eyes.

Then he feels the sun come up.

There's a knock on the door. It's Mary.

Sherry, she says.

Huh.

Get up girl we got to go. But take some shit first.

Um hmm.

Check he's got a watch.

Sherry pulls herself away from Harlan, unsticks herself from him, and gets dressed. He pretends he's asleep. She pulls the sheet over him and kisses him on the forehead and then she goes through his wallet as well as the pockets of his pants and jacket. Several hours later Sonny wakes up and finds Harlan in his bed. It takes him a few minutes to remember the events of the night before. Harlan opens his eyes and sees Sonny sitting on the edge of the mattress.

Jesus fucking Christ, Harlan says. Where am I.

You're in my bed.

Oh shit. Them girls are poison, Harlan says. I bet they cleaned us out.

They always do.

Harlan laughs. Sonny laughs too. Harlan gets up and looks around for his clothes that are balled up and still wet and now smell of mildew and he gets dressed. It's noon and Annabelle is going to be pissed because he was supposed to work on the Z28. He was supposed to keep it in his pants last night. He stands in the bathroom and looks at his bad reflection in the mirror and thinks about Annabelle. Feeling guilty, he rubs one off to her image in his mind. Then he does a couple lines with Sonny and drinks cold orange juice right from the container.

———

Annabelle wants to know where he's been. More than that, who he's been with.

I can smell that dirty pussy on you, she says.

He looks at her.

Don't think I can't, she says.

She doesn't like being kept in the dark anymore. She feels that their relationship has progressed beyond that point and if he can't get a handle on his appetite then their plan is not going to work.

Harlan listens patiently and rolls a cigarette around on his bottom lip but he doesn't light it because the landlord has a rule about smoking. All his clothes and shit are stuffed into a garbage bag and sitting by the front door. Annabelle has given him an ultimatum.

Yeah, but what about you and that Greek piece of shit, Harlan says.

That's just a money thing, Annabelle says. That's just work.

Harlan spits on the floor when she says it.

Bullshit, he says.

Get the fuck out, she says. Then she starts crying. Get your shit together or we're through, she says. Though the Greek's offer is sounding better to her every fucking day.

Harlan lets her cry a few minutes. He puts his hand on her shoulder and she gets chills and she backs away from him and throws her cup. It misses but hot coffee splashes on his leg.

Fuck, he says.

Get the fuck out.

That hurt.

You don't know hurt, she says. You son of a bitch.

Harlan grabs his gear. On the bright side this is one way of getting out of spending his afternoon under the hood of her car. His bike won't start and she's watching from the dining room window and so Harlan rolls down the hill out of her line of vision until the bike will turn over. He sits there in idle for a little while, collecting his thoughts, coming up with a plan. Then a couple hours later Lila isn't surprised to see him. She's taking out the trash and he helps her.

How long you gone to stay for this time, she says.

I don't know.

Come up for a beer when you're settled.

All right then.

Still amped from last night's coke he goes upstairs for that beer. His old man is in white boxer shorts that are stained and a white T-shirt that has yellow rings under the arms and around the neck. From his bed he's fighting Lila over something and Harlan helps get him under control.

After a while the old man settles down.

Thanks for that, she says. He doesn't have much left.

That makes your job easier.

She gets him a cold beer and they don't talk and Harlan's head hurts, and he's happy to just sit there holding Lila's hand, with his eyes closed, listening to his father's labored breathing.

On Tuesday Annabelle comes by with more of his personals.

Can we talk.

About what.

About us, she says. About our plan to fuck off out of here. You still think we can do it.

Yeah, he says.

But you got to stop with the strange pussy, she says. I just don't know what to do sometimes.

I know. But what about the fucking Greek.

Jesus. How much have you had to drink already.

Not enough.

Well, she says. So this is just a break then. A short break so you can get your mind right about our future.

Our future. All right.

He doesn't want to take a break. He imagines that fat bastard climbing on top of Annabelle, and in the next instant he imagines snapping his neck like a twig. Then he shuts his eyes and just sits there on the edge of his mattress. She wants something more from him than he is able to give, it seems. That's what it boils down to from his perspective. Annabelle stares at him and shakes her head from side to side. They can hear his old man upstairs, going into a rant. Lila's voice is calming at first but soon enough she's drowned out by a stream of booming obscenities. Annabelle never stops looking at Harlan and he finishes his drink and sucks on an ice cube and avoids her eyes. She eventually gets up and sighs and leaves.

There's a black-and-white television hooked up to power in the garage by an orange extension cord that runs through the window in the kitchenette. Harlan watches reruns of *The Price Is Right*. The reception is not so good. He only barely gets three of the local channels.

Some yahoos race old American cars down South Main. Harlan likes the way the chrome bumpers look. He stands under a tree and watches them go up the hill. Then here comes the police with the lights and sirens and everything. It looks like Westy behind the wheel, and Harlan figures those knuckleheads are lucky because he is one of the good ones at least. Then Sonny rolls up in his El Camino just out of the shop. He's listening to metal and it's cranked up really loud. Harlan flicks his cigarette butt into a pothole in the street and gets in.

Turn that shit down already, he says.

If it's too loud then you're too old.

Fuck you.

Sonny turns it down a little and then he continues to sing along and drum the steering wheel. Harlan puts his arm out the window and his head back against the sun-warmed vinyl seat.

So where in fuck we going, he says.

There's this thing I heard about. But first we got to meet Spider.

Ah that fucking guy. It sounds complicated already.

Nah.

Harlan doesn't like it when things get too complicated. He needs a drink. He knows there's always a half pint of Jim Beam in a speaker hole and he takes a couple healthy pulls from it and hands it to Sonny. Then they park in the dirt lot of the abandoned shoe factory.

They said for us to go right in, Sonny says.

Who's they, Harlan says. You said Spider.

Sonny lifts the plastic that's hanging over a side entrance and holds it up for Harlan. Come on, Sonny says again.

Harlan goes in first and Sonny follows and it takes a minute or two for their eyes to adjust. Rats scurry around and you can hear them in the shadows.

Then somebody pats them down, tells them to put their arms up, to spread their feet apart.

This is the one you told me about, another voice says.

Sonny puts his hand on Harlan's shoulder. Yeah that's right, Sonny says. This here is my man.

And together you can do this thing.

Sure we can do it.

I want to hear your friend say it.

Harlan can see now and he takes it all in. He doesn't say anything.

Cat got your tongue.

He looks at Spider, who's leaning against a doorframe.

I'm not a talker, Harlan says. That's what he does.

He nods toward Sonny.

I see, Spider says.

Harlan spits into the dust at his feet and eyeballs the bodyguard who is still looming, looking to get smacked.

Let's go, Harlan says. I don't like this one bit.

He pushes Sonny back out the way they came and Spider doesn't say anything.

Those are bad people there, Harlan says when they reach the car.

No shit.

I don't know, man. But go ahead and break it down for me.

You fight a guy or two. Five grand if you win.

Harlan looks out the window at nothing and whistles.

That's a lot of fucking scratch, he says. A guy or two, huh.

That's right. Like tournament style.

What guys.

His boys. He brings them in from the city.

Where and when.

He says we can pick a location. The weekend.

Jesus Christ.

With that kind of bread you can steal Annabelle away from that Greek fucking nigger.

Yeah, well, I guess that's the thing.

Darling Nikki isn't at her place but her roommate lets him wait inside. They smoke a blunt. Her name is Celia. She's a bohemian little thing. After an hour Nikki comes home and looks excited to see Harlan. She hugs him and sits on his lap and Celia rolls another one. They all three watch television and he rubs Darling Nikki's back and shoulders. Celia falls asleep on the floor with her mouth open and Harlan covers her with a blanket.

You're so nice, Darling Nikki says.

That's just a front.

Well your back's nice too.

Harlan laughs. He likes that she can make him laugh. Annabelle makes him laugh or at least she could when they started out but now she has put him on a break. Whatever that means.

Nikki tells him Joe isn't coming around so much anymore. He seems to be getting the hint, she says. And she has a line on a duplex in Greenfield. It's a good place for her right now.

I'm in a good place, she says. And I have you to thank.

Well, go ahead and thank me already.

She works him from the outside of his pants with her hand. Then she unzips his fly and leads him like that to her room. Her dog is sleeping on a pillow on the floor and he looks up. Harlan makes a comment about performance anxiety in front of an audience and Darling Nikki laughs and shoos Bushy from the room and locks her door.

My poor baby, she says.

Him or me.

Him, because you're about to be all right.

She gets on her knees and undoes his pants and he watches the top of her head move up and down for several minutes until he finally relaxes and she even stays down there so that there isn't a mess. She looks up at him and then lets go his ass cheeks.

Where'd you learn that, he says.

Some things you don't need to learn.

Is that right.

Like you with the fights, she says, standing. Just comes natural.

Then she pushes him playfully back onto the twin mattress that she uses. It doesn't have a box spring. She catches him by surprise and he actually does lose his balance. He struggles through a brief bout with vertigo.

Not so tough now, she says.

Never said I was.

No you didn't, she says. But everybody else did.

Lila is outside having a smoke and Harlan bums one off of her. She can't smoke inside because of the oxygen tanks. They joke about what a mess that would make and Harlan even pictures it in his mind. Together they watch the full moon rise round and perfect. It's that curious time of day when the sun and the moon are in the sky at the same time. That nothing time caught between day and night. Not quite one or the other. Harlan's favorite part of the day, in fact.

A blood-red sunset is draped over Mount Toby.

I had to call the volunteers the other day, she says. Everything just stopped. His heart and everything. He wasn't even breathing.

So that was it.

Maybe, Lila says. Almost.

Harlan looks at his old man.

I panicked, she says. I called Boho and the fire truck came.

They generally do. Harlan looks at Lila and she looks away from him.

They brought him back like but took him to Cooley Dick to make sure, she says.

Should've just let him go like that, Harlan says. He doesn't mean to upset her but she cries just the same. I mean that wouldn't be too bad a way to go, he says.

I thought of that afterward. Of you. I knew you'd say that, she says. I looked for you downstairs.

I was out.

You were out, she says. You're always out. So they kept him overnight for observation. I just got him back.

How is he now.

Same as always.

Harlan can smell his father. Lila cries some more. Harlan just stands there and lets her get it all out.

Bitch gives him warts and he's not even sure which one. A small doctor with a foreign accent and delicate brown hands freezes them off Harlan's pecker. He's going to quit all the others, Sally and Nikki and whatever else pussy gets thrown his way. He doesn't need it anymore. It's become a hassle more than anything, and Annabelle wants to escape with him—that's how she termed it. Escape to Vermont or New Hampshire or where-the-fuck-ever. Escape from the fighting and the stripping and the whoring.

We're both whores, she'd said to him one time when they were just starting out together. And so how did we end up like this, she'd said.

How could we not, was all he could think.

But they've each managed to save a bit of scratch, although he doesn't know what else he'd do once they got there, wherever. He figures he could get a job doing roadwork if there are any such jobs left.

I don't want to go somewhere new and do the same shit, he said.

Yeah, I'm done with this wrong life, too, she said.

She said it like she meant it but Harlan wasn't convinced they could either one of them pull it off. Even back then it had seemed like a fucking pipe dream. And now they're on a break.

He calls her on the phone.

Anyhow, he says.

So anyhow I'm going away for a few days, she said. It's no big deal.

The Greek takes Annabelle to Atlantic City. They stay at the Trump Towers and he plays blackjack until five in the morning. Annabelle gets bored and wanders around the casino, people watching. When they meet back at the room she's hammered and says he can do whatever he wants as long as he hurries. But what he wants is for her to use toys on herself while he squeezes his own juice out. It doesn't take long. The next day she drinks watered-down Mai Tais by the shitty little pool. There's a group of professional bowlers lounging on the cement deck. They try to get her attention but she's good at ignoring drunk rednecks. Finally one gets up the balls to approach her, and he's all right, but she tells him to fuck off and so he does. His buddies laugh at him and speculate aloud about her sexual preferences. She shuts her eyes and tunes out all the noise and she thinks about Harlan. He said he was going to kill the fucking Greek.

She believes that he will, that he can, but she is more worried for him than for the other one.

He'd do it for sure if he knew she was with him right now.

She shouldn't have mentioned the casino trip to Harlan. She saw it as her chance to get away and think. And she doesn't blame Harlan for being pissed, but she had explained that there are some definite pluses to what the Greek has put on the table; she'll be living in a nice pad rent-free, so she can stop dancing for money and focus on her poetry, for example. And the Greek's various connections in the printing industry might be able to help get her work published. These are the things he has promised her. The downside of course is that he is a disgusting pig and she's going to have to let him ravage her a couple times a week. But she's been there before. She can handle that. There's a place she goes inside her head where nobody can touch her. She learned about that special place as a young girl and can transport herself there with the blink of an eye. But Harlan can't stand the thought of her being with another man like that. It drives him crazy.

We can still be together, she'd said.

He'll never even know, she'd said. Nothing will ever change between us.

But they both know that is a huge crock of shit.

———

Harlan's hands are hard as marble. He hits the dude's jaw so square it feels like a bag of sand. Sonny cheers. Spider from the shoe factory and his bodyguard are there to watch, even though they don't usually get many spectators. He nods in approval but Harlan ignores him. It's the last one of the night and Sonny collects the money from everybody. Then he speaks to Spider but Harlan doesn't hear what they are saying, doesn't even want to know. He puts a clean T-shirt on and drinks a shot of warm whiskey. He sits on an old stool that is peeling paint.

He coughs blood.

Sonny gives him most of the money. That's the deal. Nice work, Sonny says. Hey, our friend was impressed.

Your fucking friend.

Whatever.

Harlan spits more blood and puts his head in his hands. He feels around his mouth with his tongue for a loose tooth. He spits it on the cement floor.

That night Annabelle stops by his father's place and says she wants him back.

I thought we were on break. You and the Greek and whatnot.

Fuck that, she says. I miss you.

Lila snorts. She's sitting on Harlan's bed with him. She'd brought him aspirin and orange juice and he's drinking it. Annabelle looks at Lila and dismisses her with a wave of her hand like to call her a skanky old bitch.

Well, she says to Harlan.

Well what.

You coming or what.

Where in fuck you been.

I went to Atlantic City with him. You remember.

You can't just waltz in here with his cock on your breath.

Annabelle can't believe what she's hearing. She'd convinced herself that Harlan had been pining away for her. She looks at Harlan and at Lila, then back at Harlan. A light bulb goes on in her head.

She has convinced herself of something else now.

You got to be shitting me, she says. Are you banging your father's ass-wiper.

Jesus fucking Christ, Harlan says.

Lila snorts again and drinks her orange juice in three gulps. There's something else in there too that gets her through the day, most days anyhow.

That's it, Annabelle says. He's dying up there and you're fucking this washed-up bitch, she says. Splitting his social security probably.

Lila stands up.

You always said that's all she was after, Annabelle says.

Lila balls up her little hand and throws it at Annabelle. It hits her in the face and takes her completely by surprise but doesn't do much damage at all.

Harlan gets up and bum rushes Annabelle before she can react. He practically carries her to her Z28, puts her inside. Get the fuck out of here, he says.

You cocksucker. I'm with the fucking Greek then.

As soon as she says it Harlan wants to pound on somebody. It hurts to hear those words. The hell you are, he says.

She starts the engine and pops the clutch and has to start it again. Harlan watches until she's around the corner and he can't hear her grinding the Z28's gears anymore.

Lila is crying inside.

Sorry about that, he says.

Oh, that's not on you, she says. I never did like that one.

Yeah.

It's not the money, you know. I don't want you to think that's what it is, she says. The only thing.

I know.

Did you really say that.

Well, I don't mean half what I say.

I mean it does help, she says. The checks. I won't lie. It helps me some days when he's really awful, she says. To think about it.

All right, Harlan says. You don't have to explain nothing, I know how the world works.

I didn't even know about it at first, she says. That he even had a pot to piss in. Then when I found out he was already in such bad shape.

Come here. He hugs Lila as best he can and she shivers against him.

It wouldn't be so bad, would it, she says.

What's that now, he says.

You and me.

Ah, he says, looking over her head out the window. He has never seen the sky so fucking blue. Sometimes there's God, he thinks, as a swarm of black crows alights just beyond the grain silo in the field across the way and other kinds of birds sit on a telephone wire that alternatively stretches and sags above Route 5. Harlan doesn't even want his old man's money. Lila can have it all. The house and the money and every-fucking-thing. He figures she deserves it. She's the one who has kept him out of the hospital or the nursing home or the graveyard. She's the one who has taken all the abuse, replacing his mother. Harlan likes Lila and never really thought that she was just in it for the checks.

Mary asks Sonny for some nose candy.

Nobody calls it that anymore, he says.

Whatever, she says. You know what I mean.

The great white snake, he smartasses.

Let's chase the great white snake then.

What do I get in return.

What do you want.

Sonny laughs his laugh because she knows exactly what he wants.

There's a zip lock bag in his sock drawer and he sets up a couple fat lines for her on the glass top of his coffee table. She uses a credit card to straighten them out and then hoovers them up her nose.

Where's your sister at.

What you want with her.

Nothing. I'm just asking.

We're not talking right now, Mary says. That bitch has mental problems, she says.

Sonny takes a couple quick toots just to be sociable. I'm supposed to meet Harlan, he says. Want to come, he asks.

Where.

The Bloody Brook.

That fucking place.

Yeah. I know.

All right.

Mary sits right up against him in the car, like they're going for couple of the year. It feels good to him when she does that.

This is like high school music, she says. What is this shit.

Creedence Clearwater.

Jesus Christ, she says. That's right.

Sonny opens the glove box and fumbles around with some tapes. Mary takes them from him and looks them over and snickers. She looks at one and then drops it on the floor and then does the same with the next. Then she starts fooling with the radio dial, cruising the airwaves for something good.

Boy, you are out of touch, she says.

There's nothing wrong with those, he says. And you better pick them up.

She picks up the cassettes and puts them back carefully. I'm just saying, she says. That shit's old as fuck.

She knows he's in a bad way now and so she rubs his leg until he relaxes and then she puts on a station he likes. Sonny shakes his head, enjoys the way she's grooving in her seat. Then they're out in the street and Sonny hits her. But it isn't that hard and it won't even leave a mark. In his mind, the problem is that she's a fucking drama queen. He considers it more of a love tap than anything but she's screaming bloody murder. And of course he has to shut her up. It isn't like she hasn't been touched like that before. It isn't a new thing to her, getting knocked around a bit. So Sonny doesn't understand why she's getting all excited. When she finally calms down he tries to help her stand up but she just stays huddled against the curb, sobbing.

He looks around to make sure nobody's being nosy.

Keep your trap shut about this, he says.

Fuck you.

Sonny can't believe how disrespectful she still is. He pulls his leg back to give her a good one in the rib cage and she balls up, and lucky for her he changes his mind at the last second.

You bring it on yourself with that mouth of yours, he says.

He gets two beers from a cooler in the back of the El Camino and pops them open and offers one to her. She won't even look at him. He drinks his and then he drinks hers too. He looks at her again. Mary looks up from what is now a sitting position and keeps quiet.

See, now that's better, he says.

Mary sniffles.

Sometimes you just got to know when to shut the hell up, girl.

Sonny puts seven ice cubes from the cooler in the Ziploc bag he'd used for coke and he scoops Mary up off the street. She makes him so angry sometimes. The way she laughs at him isn't like he's in on the joke at all and that's almost always what pushes him over the edge.

You just need to check yourself, is all.

She looks at him this time and stays looking at him for a long time. She half smiles.

Fuck you, she says.

But he does love her spunk. She's a little spitfire. You're going to be all right, he says.

She's in a certain amount of pain and he hates to see that but he also knows deep in his heart that there are some hard lessons that have to be taught. He tells her about these lessons and how it's good for her in the long run. She moans, puts her head on him.

It's about respect and it's about knowing your place.

She nods her head up and down and he strokes her dark hair.

I hate when you make me get like that, he says. When you make me do like that.

I'm sorry, she says.

I don't know why you do that, he says.

She apologizes again and he cradles her just like he might a baby or a small child and she wonders if he'll be a good daddy someday.

Spider is connected. That's what Sonny says when he meets Harlan at the Bloody Brook. No shit, Sherlock, Harlan says back. Sonny is thinking maybe he can help with the Greek. But the truth of the matter is Sonny has troubles of his own where he could use a boost. In debt up to his eyeballs. There were some ventures that hadn't proved as successful as he had hoped. The comic book store. The sandwich place. The coffee shop in Greenfield. He always has good ideas and he has balls enough to get things going but his problem is that he isn't a finisher. He's had a good run on the horses, though, and he plays poker at the Polish Club most Friday nights and he has the backwoods fight scene working pretty good. But he never gets his head above water.

Sonny meets with Spider. He doesn't bring Harlan along because he's being such a wet blanket about the whole damn thing. They drink coffee at the pharmacy.

You play, Spider says, indicating the chessboard on a nearby table, and when Sonny says he doesn't Spider asks why not.

I don't know. I'm too impatient, I guess.

It's a wonderful game, Spider tells him. Not unlike fighting.

But it's so fucking boring.

It's strategy. For both, it's strategy that wins.

Sonny thinks he's crazy but he doesn't mind crazy much. Spider explains that there are serious consequences if they back out now. Once the ball is rolling and expectations are set.

Got it, Sonny says.

There's lots of details, Spider says.

Sonny is happy and relieved to not have to worry about the details.

Harlan is nowhere to be found. Sonny checks his old man's house and the Conway Inn and Mike's Westview, where he likes to go sometimes when it isn't too crowded with all the damn college kids. He even takes a ride into Turners Falls to see if he's with Annabelle.

Why would he be here, she says.

I don't know, Sonny says. Why fucking not.

Annabelle's making coffee and invites him in for some. He follows her to the kitchen. She isn't wearing much, just an old T-shirt and a pair of pink cotton underpants that are going up her butt. She uses a finger to pick them out while she pours him a cup with the other hand and he watches and she catches him looking. She smiles at him, and Sonny sure knows what she's thinking, what she's up to here, and that is simply out of the question. Not that he would mind. To her it would be a sweet form of revenge perhaps, but to him it would be the same as suicide.

Well, she says. He doesn't stay here anymore.

That's what I heard.

She looks at him. What else did you hear.

Her voice has turned bitter and he knows he has to walk on those eggshells now. Just that you were taking a break.

My ass, she says. That motherfucker is two-timing me.

Sonny laughs and the steam of the coffee soothes the skin of his face where he shaved.

What's funny, Annabelle says.

He shakes his head at himself for being so stupid. Nothing, he says. Nothing's funny. He's nuts about you is all.

Well, she says. He has a different way of showing it.

Yeah, you know how he is.

They drink their coffees and she stands even closer to him now.

Look at me, she says.

It takes everything in him to not look at her.

What are you scared of, she says. She puts her empty cup down and stands right up against him. She runs her hand up his leg and she can feel how excited he is. Maybe scared's not the word, she says.

Sonny finishes his drink and gently pushes her away from him but she holds his arm.

Come on, Sonny, she says. I see how you look at me.

Looking's one thing, he says.

She takes his hand and places it on her and she pushes her pelvic bone against him.

Are we gone to do this, she says, or what.

He keeps his hand there for a little while. Yeah, he sure as shit knows what she's up to here. He's tempted but he considers the consequences and whether or not it would be worth it. He's on the fence when lucky for him the phone rings and breaks him out of her trance.

Annabelle goes to the phone.

Yeah hello, she says.

Sonny puts his mug on the counter.

Oh hey, she says. The fuck you want. Then she pauses. Yeah, he's here right now, looking for you as a matter of fact, she says, fake smiling at Sonny. We were just having a nice chat, she adds before handing Sonny the phone.

Sonny takes the call in the living room so she can't listen. Harlan wants to hook up for a beer. He doesn't sound pissed but something is definitely wrong. He doesn't even ask what Sonny is doing at Annabelle's.

How'd you know I was here.

Lila said you came by and were headed there next. He says, Just meet me at the Inn, and hangs up.

Sonny hands the phone back to Annabelle, who snatches it from him and slams it back into the cradle. She puts her hands on her hips and cocks one of them to the side. Well, she says.

Well what.

What did that motherfucker want.

Just looking for me, Sonny says. We're gone to get a beer.

He didn't say nothing about me.

Nope, he says. What's there to say.

That no-good prick, she says. So you're gone to see him now.

Yeah, I'm gone.

Then let him smell me on you, she thinks, flipping hair out of her face and giving him the puppy-dog eyes. He sees it coming from a long mile away. She peels off her shirt over her head and she's not wearing any kind of bra.

Sonny thanks her for the coffee and tries to slide past her to the front door. She follows him and even grabs hold of his collar, and he tries to duck and squirm away.

He really does try.

Harlan is waiting for Sonny out in front of the Conway Inn, having a smoke. What took you, he says.

That girl of yours.

What about her.

She's a real pistol is all.

They go inside the bar. Sonny considers telling Harlan what happened back there in Turners but he can't see any good coming from it. Except if he doesn't say shit now, Annabelle might try to turn it around on him and make it look bad so Harlan would side with her. In that case it would be better to come clean up front, he figures. But he doesn't think she'll do that. And even though Sonny has never given Harlan any reason to mistrust him, he decides then and there to clam up about the whole thing. He'll tell the whole truth later if it comes down to that.

Did she make a run at you, Harlan says.

Sonny swallows some beer wrong and Harlan slaps him on the back. Jesus, Sonny says. What'd you say.

That's her thing when she's pissed at me, Harlan says. Then she uses it to get at me, you know.

I hope you know I'd never.

I know, Harlan says. But she's got me all twisted.

Sonny fingers the bowl of stale nuts and pretzels.

The rain is coming down so hard that it's also going up. Sonny is drunk now and he watches Harlan fumble with his bike behind the bar. It's no use. He's in no condition to ride anyhow. But there's no talking to Harlan sometimes and Sonny stands there and watches him and eventually Harlan curses and gives up just as a Cadillac edges alongside them. The window comes down a crack and it's Spider inside. He has a couple black girls with him, probably from Holyoke, and a bottle of brown booze in his clutch. He opens the door and Sonny and Harlan get in. It's warm and dry and the stereo is playing some kind of jazzy shit.

My two friends, Spider says. We're looking for you.

The girls giggle. They're all over Spider and it's clear he has agreed to pay them.

So this is how you train for a fight, he says.

Harlan looks at Spider and he looks at each of the girls and he looks at Sonny. Shit, he says.

What you mean.

What I mean is shit, Harlan says.

Sonny laughs. The girls giggle. Spider says something to the girls and they laugh at whatever it is. The driver laughs too and then parks across the street. Harlan pushes against the door, gets out of the car.

Let's have a little party together, Spider says.

Sonny follows Harlan into the rain and stands in front of him. Come on, Sonny says. Just a few more drinks.

I don't like it, Harlan says. Don't like that guy.

Come on.

Harlan sways. He's having a hard time keeping his balance and Sonny helps him.

Shit, I haven't seen you this bad in I don't know how long. He steers Harlan to the front door of the Inn and Spider and the girls follow them back inside. They sit at a round table and Sonny lets Harlan fall asleep with his head on it. Spider gets one of the girls to sit with Sonny and rub his leg. Her warm tongue darts in and out of his ear like a hummingbird.

Maybe it's better your friend is drunk, Spider says.

Sonny looks at Harlan.

You and me, we share the pussy tonight, he says.

Sonny raises his glass and there is a funky foursome making its way slowly to the stage. They are old and white-haired but once they start playing rock and roll it doesn't much matter. Spider dances. He twirls his whore around the floor and she throws her head back and laughs like a debutante. Sonny dances with his girl too and when he sits back down Harlan is long fucking gone. Sonny looks at the driver.

Where'd he go, he says.

The driver ignores him and stares straight ahead.

Where the fuck is he.

Spider barks at the driver and gets a terse response. Then he turns and faces Sonny and he smiles but not nice.

Your friend, he left, he says. Now it's just us.

Sonny finds Harlan at his father's house. They are both hung and Harlan is lying on the bed and Sonny is on the floor. Lila is making a pot of coffee, says they smell like a whiskey mill.

Is there even a whiskey mill anymore, Sonny says.

I guess there is.

Where they actually make the whiskey, Sonny says. At a mill.

That's the official term, Lila says.

Shit, Harlan says. Who the fuck cares.

Well, she said it like she knew what she was talking about.

People say all kinds of things with authority.

Sonny looks away. Where'd you end up last night, he says.

Here.

Was the ride all right.

I don't know, Harlan says. I woke up and I was here.

When did you leave.

I don't remember leaving anywhere.

We are at the Inn dancing and then you were gone.

Dancing, Harlan says. I don't dance.

Not you, Sonny says. Me and Spider and them spades.

Harlan doesn't remember any of it. He'd had one of his spells. He doesn't remember seeing Spider. Sonny laughs and Lila comes back with two cups of coffee with milk.

Here you go, boys.

Thanks, Lila.

Yeah, thanks.

She leans against the doorframe and watches them. Maybe we can talk later, she says to Harlan.

Sure, Harlan says. What about.

Your father.

What about him.

Let's do it later, she says. If that's okay.

Sonny gets up. I can leave if you want, he says.

No that's okay, Lila says. You boys rest.

Lila goes back up to the house. Sonny sits down.

Harlan closes his eyes and squeezes them. There's no aspirin anywhere. The ghost of the old man starts screaming upstairs and there's some light leaking through the garage and into the room where Lila left the door open a little bit, dust particles floating in the beam and looking almost religious. Harlan starts to snore and Sonny removes the mug from his hand so he won't spill hot coffee on himself. He decides to wait until Harlan wakes up and then he'll tell him the fight is scheduled for Tuesday next.

When he hears Annabelle's voice, Harlan thinks he's dreaming.

What the fuck happened, she says.

There it is again. Harlan opens his eyes. Annabelle is crying.

Look at you, she says.

He tries to speak but something is wrong with his mouth. He sits up and looks around. It's Annabelle's apartment. Everything is all busted up, blood and pieces of broken glass and furniture everywhere. A kitchen knife with a busted blade on the floor nearby.

What the fuck did you do, she says.

His memory is coming back. It's not a dream. Tuesday night, after he beat Spider's guys, both of them, he came to get Annabelle and that Greek fuck was in her apartment and they both started yelling and throwing hands. That's all he can remember before the fog settles back in.

I think he's dead, Annabelle says. We got to get out of here.

She helps him stand. His left leg doesn't work much so he drags it along. Annabelle's Z28 is out front and she puts him in the backseat and he lies down to rest because he's so tired. The car starts after two or three tries and he can smell the gas because she almost flooded it.

Don't pump the gas so much, he says.

What the fuck, she says.

You got the money.

Yeah. Sonny gave it to me.

Good. It's for you.

Jesus. I think he stabbed you in a couple places.

You can go somewhere nice with that much cash.

Oh, baby. Don't talk like that.

Like what.

There's no place nice without you.

He feels along his upper thigh and it seems she's right about him being stabbed. A homemade bandage is in place, an old T-shirt. Some fucking girl, he thinks. But she's driving too fast so he tells her slow down because it doesn't matter now. None of it does. She's talking, but her voice is slipping away from him. He tries to curl up into a ball in his seat but the pain is finally too much, where he got stuck in the gut too, and so he closes his eyes. He pictures a simple farmhouse on maybe twenty acres, a horse or two, and a big red barn.

FurtherMore

ABOUT THE AUTHOR

- A Conversation with Jon Boilard

ABOUT THE BOOK

"The characters in these stories have been haunting me for years. That's why I wrote them down."

READ ON

- Bonus Story

ABOUT THE AUTHOR

Jon Boilard was born and raised in Western Massachusetts, and he has been living in Northern California since 1986. His award-winning short stories have appeared in some of the finest literary journals in the United States, Canada, Europe, and Asia.

Jon's debut short story collection, *Settright Road* (Dzanc Books, 2017), is preceded by two novels, *The Castaway Lounge* (Dzanc Books, 2015) and *A River Closely Watched* (MacAdam Cage, 2012). ARCW was a finalist for the Northern California Book Award. He has participated in the Cork International Short Story Festival in Cork, Ireland, the Wroclaw Short Story Festival in Wroclaw, Poland, and LitQuake in San Francisco, California.

Jon currently resides in the Sunset District of San Francisco with his wife and two daughters.

A CONVERSATION WITH JON BOILARD

Why do you write?

I write because I have to write. It's just how I make sense of the world, and how I sort through my own personal shit. Writing fiction to me is certainly not a hobby and it's not a part-time job, even though I treat it that way in terms of how I set aside time and prepare myself for a session. And it's not a passion either—more along the lines of a compulsion. Quite frankly, if I don't write for a few days, my head gets all fucked up. I simply must write. I imagine it's cheaper than therapy.

You tend to write stories that are full of dark characters and scenes. Do you ever become so engulfed in that world that you struggle to re-emerge into your own?

That happens for sure when I'm working on a story. Because I do tend to write about these dark characters, or at least people who are in trouble or whose souls are in danger—sometimes it's good people in bad situations. And it is easy for me to get lost in that world. I was talking to creative writing students at the international short story festival in Wroclaw, Poland, just last year, and I compared the process to what I imagine actors go through when they get into character, how challenging it must be to then slip out of character and go back to normal life. Daniel Day-Lewis comes to mind—how he throws himself into his craft and basically becomes the character he's portraying. That takes a physical and mental toll, slipping into and out of those dark places.

So that part of the writing process is difficult for me. The journey can be scary and exhausting because you can learn things about yourself. Don't get me wrong on this point; it's a thrill to be able to do it, invigorating when it works the way it's supposed to. When everything clicks just right, there's nothing more exhilarating. And like any other addict, I simply have to go back for more. But the reality is sometimes I get stuck in a middle place, a holding cell, between worlds and I have to chase the demons back and there are some healthy ways that I do that and there are some other very unhealthy ones, too.

During the day, when you are going about your normal activities and some aspect of a story comes into your head, do you need to stop and record a few thoughts, or do your ideas hang around for you to tackle later?

They stay in my head, haunting me throughout the day. Typically my writing time is early in the morning, between 4 a.m. and 6 a.m., so that's when I put stuff down on paper. I don't carry a notepad around or anything like that. But the ideas are constantly knocking around in my brain, distracting me, keeping me off balance.

Between 4 a.m. and 6 a.m.? That's an early start...

It is early, and to be honest, 4 a.m. comes a lot faster now than it did even ten years ago. By 8 a.m. I've got my daughters dropped at school and I'm on the M train heading downtown to the office for the day job. I usually do my best stuff early in the morning, when I first wake up. Sometimes I've got some big idea that I need to get down on paper and sometimes it's just a matter of reviewing the previous day's work. The house is really quiet and still at that hour, just me and the dog are up, and I need that kind of stillness when I write. I like to crack a window open so I can hear the foghorn in the San Francisco Bay.

It's a very blue-collar approach to craft, rising early to get after it, which makes sense, I suppose, considering my background, my work-a-day New England roots. To me the important thing is to punch in mentally and physically, to get my ass in the chair and shut everything else out and be ready when the muse stops by for a visit. She can be very elusive, so I want to be prepared or at least available.

What about location? Where do you write, or does it even matter?

It matters a lot. Location is pretty important to me. I am such a damn robot, a creature of habit. If you take me out of my routine, I can get rattled. There is a small room attached to the garage. That's typically where I bang out my stories, where I do the bulk of the really tangible, hands-on writing.

But having said that, there is a part of my process that is at least equally important and that I do anywhere and everywhere. Once I get an idea for a story or a character stuck in my head, I noodle on it constantly. This drives the people in my life crazy because I can become very distant and distracted in all other aspects of the day-to-day. So a lot of the pre-work is done inside my head while I'm driving on 101 or running the dog on the beach or mixing a drink or whatever. My older daughter likes to tease me that I'm not very observant, which is funny, and I have explained to her that the stuff I observe or pay attention to is just different than what normal people would care about or notice.

Not to get too hung up on process, but how do you write short stories? Longhand?

For years I was a pen-and-notepad guy, a longhand guy. I'm such a terrible typist (I still hunt and peck) that it just didn't make sense to get in front of a keyboard until the very last minute. But as I've grown as a writer, it has become clear to me that I do much of the writing inside my head anyhow.

When I finally do sit down at my laptop now, it's really to spit a short story out, to record it. It's already mostly developed and just needs some tinkering here and there, and that process plays well with my two-finger typing because it's slow going and allows me to ponder every word. The process is a bit different for longer pieces, but that holds true for the short stories.

How do your memories of growing up in small New England towns feed your creative process?

We moved to South Deerfield, Massachusetts, when I was twelve years old. During my years at Frontier Regional High School, I worked on farms picking tobacco and cucumbers and at the gas station in the center of town. I was a full-fledged townie boy, and I got to know a lot of people. One of the big comments I heard from some of these folks back home, when they read my first novel, was, "It's like you grew up in a different town than I grew up in. I don't know that part of town you're talking about."

I recognize the apparent disconnect there. Most of my stories reveal these rough and desperate little river towns, but a lot of my memories from childhood are actually that sort of Norman Rockwell feel. I mean, I loved growing up there. But because of how my first twelve years were spent, there was a fair amount of abuse and neglect, so I understood—I could see—that there were other things going on, behind closed doors. I was wary. My brother and I, we could pick up on signals that most kids our age wouldn't probably pick up on.

In my work, I do tend to contrast the natural beauty of rural New England with the messy lives of my characters.

I remember a reviewer referred to your first novel as a "poison pen letter to your former home." How do you react to that?

That's bullshit. I go back home whenever I can. I take my wife and daughters in the summer and we swim in the Deerfield River. I have stayed close with many of my friends who are still back home.

Even though I really only lived in South Deerfield for six years, I still think of it as my hometown and feel a strong connection there. My brother is buried back there, too, so of course so we visit his grave and I tell the girls stories about some of the less insane shit we used to do when we were just a little bit older than they are. The older my daughters get, the better the stories get.

Talk about being a townie.

We lived in town, worked in town, raised a fair amount of hell in town. After school and on weekends, I worked at the service station pumping gas and learning cars. My buddy worked across the street, stocking shelves at the pharmacy, and we had another good friend, a few years older, who worked at the package store. So we pretty much had the center of town covered. Our friend at the packy would sell us beer out the back door so we could drive around and drink. You had to have a car. As soon as you got your license, you had to be on the road.

During the summer, we worked on the farms, picking every kind of vegetable you can think of and some tobacco, throwing bales of hay. It was physical work, hard work. There were other kids whose families were maybe better off financially and they didn't have to work, and I'm sure we thought it sucked at the time, having to get up early and bust our asses all day out in the fields. But looking back, I think we learned a lot about life and responsibility out there.

What was your first car?

It was a 1973 Chevy Nova. It wasn't mint condition, but it was all I could afford and it looked pretty cool. I bought it about six months before I was to get my license and threw a coat of paint on it, got some nice chrome rims. The previous owner had been in an accident and had to replace the fender so it said 307, which told you how big the engine was. So a 307 is a V8, which is pretty fast. But that replacement fender was a lie, because my car only had a straight-six 250, not much get-up-and-go at all. I remember my boss at the service station saying that it was the perfect car for me because he knew I was driving around drinking, trying to show off for pretty girls. I guess he figured a slow car would keep me out of trouble.

I sold the Nova to some young kid in town when I graduated—I was selling all my stuff to raise money for my trip west. I guess he only drove it for a few months before it shit the bed and ended up at the junkyard, which I hate to admit made me happy. I didn't want some kid driving around town in my car.

Why did you move to San Francisco?

A little while back, I watched an old video where Frank O'Connor talked about his relationship with his hometown of Cork. The way he described it was that the maturity level of Cork for him was eighteen years old. In other words, once he turned eighteen, there wasn't anything left for him there. He stayed away for a long while and even spent a bunch of time here in the States and caught a certain amount of shit for abandoning Cork. As he got older and more mature, he sort of drifted back to his hometown and embraced it, and I think it embraced him too.

When I graduated high school, I could've stayed on at the service station where I'd been working or maybe gone to a local college. I was pretty decent at school but never a great student. And I wasn't ever any good at wrenching on cars or pounding nails or farming—those are the guys who have been successful. Lots of my friends went into long careers in law enforcement. That just wasn't me, so I headed west when my dad and stepmom offered to help me out. During the college years, I got part-time gigs in a warehouse or waiting tables, but I'd go back home every summer to work construction and make some real money. When I finished up at State, I stuck around because by then I had made some friends and we were still young and dumb for the most part, hitting the bars and having a hell of a time.

Favorite bars in San Francisco?

Back then it was Holy Cow, the Boathouse, and Bottom of the Hill—or anywhere there was a good band playing and some pretty girls. Truth be told, I don't get after it much anymore, but nowadays if I am able to sneak out for a few pops I will go to Gino & Carlo's, Maggie McGarry's, or the Philosopher's Club. The key for me is to have a great bartender, somebody who can really shoot the shit. Maggie's has karaoke on Wednesday nights. I'm no performer, but I get a kick out of the people with balls enough to do it.

Where do you get your ideas?

I'll be sitting in a bar and maybe the guy next to me says something that kick-starts me for whatever reason. I'll sort of study him perched there on his stool and build some context around whatever he just said. Maybe I'll hear people talking on Muni. There are some fascinating people out there. Ideas are everywhere. Snippets of conversation like that, something in the newspaper, a memory from my own life.

Finding ideas isn't the challenge. The challenge for me is figuring out which ideas are worth developing right now, which should be put on the back burner, which should be tossed aside forever. And, of course, how to marry an idea with the other elements of fiction.

What advice do you give to young writers out there?

I used to write speeches for a guy who started a mutual fund company back in the 1950s. Today it's one of the top names, among the biggest and most respected players out there. Incredibly successful. That was one of my first non-blue-collar jobs, and even though I haven't done any work for the man for a several years, I still have a lot of respect for him and what he was able to build from scratch.

I remember a little plaque on his desk with a quote from Calvin Coolidge: "Nothing in the world can take the place of persistence. Talent will not; nothing is more common than unsuccessful men with talent. Genius will not; unrewarded genius is almost a proverb. Education will not; the world is full of educated derelicts. Persistence and determination alone are omnipotent."

My old boss meant to apply the lesson to a life in business, but it really resonated with me as far as working on my craft. Ironically, it was this exact sentiment that inspired me to quit that company after twelve years and go off and try to finish my first novel. Plus I got into a major pissing contest with another guy at the company who was way more ambitious than I was, but that's a story for another day.

Persistence and determination. That's great advice for young writers.

What's next? What are you working on now?

I'm working on a new novel that right now I'm calling *Among the Broken Pines*. I'd say I'm probably about a quarter of the way through it as of today, based on word count alone. It's dark and gritty and in line with what I've seen referred to as my tendency for New England Gothic. The opening scene is a kid throwing a child molester off the roof of his house. I'm also pulling together another collection of short stories, but these ones take place in San Francisco and abroad, so that'll be a little bit of a different deal. There's always something cooking.

ABOUT THE BOOK

On the Title

We actually lived on Settright Road. That was the first place we lived when we moved to South Deerfield to stay with my uncle and his girlfriend at the time. And my brother and I would cross the street in the morning—we'd get up early, before anybody else—and the cows were there, and the cornfields went on forever, and the fresh air was kind of like, "Everything's going to be all right." There were some more twists and turns, of course, but that was really the start of something for me and Carl. So the name has stayed with me, and I eventually figured it might make a great title for a short story and maybe even a book or a movie or a television series. One of the stories in the collection is called "Settright Road"; it's about a kid dealing with the death of his brother, told in the second person.

On the Characters

The characters in these stories have been haunting me for years. That's why I wrote them down.

For a handful of years, my uncle taught poetry and short story writing at a jail in Massachusetts. His students were typically guys who were going to be in the system a while because they had done some pretty horrible shit. Morally questionable shit. He used to share my short stories with his class, as well as my novels, and my work really resonated with them. They'd tell my uncle during workshops that they recognized themselves in my characters, they saw their own stories in my stories, and they appreciated that I didn't judge them. And they wanted to know how I knew so much about what they called "the life."

I have always figured I am maybe one or two bad decisions away from being in their shoes. If you look at how these guys were raised up compared to how I was raised up—pretty similar childhood experiences. Abuse of all stripes, neglect, fucked-up adults showing you all the wrong things. But then I got lucky and some good folks stepped in at critical points in my life and got me going in the right direction. Not everybody gets so lucky.

I do understand how a guy can get off track and desperate and maybe even hopeless and end up in jail or worse. I think his story is worth telling, I think we can learn from it. Don't get me wrong on this point: having a shitty childhood doesn't give a person license to go around doing dirt on others. But I feel a certain amount of empathy there.

The characters I created for *Settright Road* are pure fiction, but I did sometimes pluck traits from people I know or have met or bumped into. Rather than create the characters in order to serve the stories I was trying to tell, the characters came first and then I put them in situations and developed stories to serve as their platforms. The characters always showed up first.

Just to be clear, because I get this question a lot, these short stories are not true stories or necessarily based on things I did or experienced. For example, I've never choked a guy out like Sean in "Storm Chaser." I've never busted a guy in the head with a pipe like Jabber in "Watch Out, Townie Boy." But I like to say there is an emotional truth in each one of the pieces.

On the Stories

Most of the stories in this collection are pretty short, usually around five hundred to fifteen hundred words, except for "Sometimes There's God," which is the last story in the book and just about ten thousand words. The shortest one in *Settright Road* is "I Won't Wear Black," weighing in at less than three hundred words. I don't sit down to write a story with a word count in mind; I simply write it until it's finished.

Trying to figure out what stories fit together for this collection was another challenge for me, because I wrote each piece as a stand-alone, not thinking about a book. I remember hearing a writer I admire say that, for her, putting together a short story collection was like weaving a quilt, where you have a patchwork of smaller pieces coming together to form a larger, layered one. You can't just slap them all together and start stitching. With *Settright Road*, the editor and I put lot of thought into what story should go where as far as pacing and shifting tones.

On Making Time

It is rare that I have a full day I can dedicate to writing fiction, since I've got a real job as well as a young family. So by necessity I'm a short-burst guy, a sprinter for sure. The key for me is that I sprint every day. I worked on my first novel full time for eighteen months, but that was definitely the exception and not the rule. I was in between corporate gigs back then and had some money saved up, so figured what the hell. And it was cool being able to do that, write fiction full time. I treated it like a nine-to-five job, packed a lunch pail, mostly set up shop at a noisy little café down by Ocean Beach. It was great.

But the demands of raising a family in San Francisco require a steady paycheck, that's just how it is, and so until I start selling a crapload more books I'll continue to do the corporate writing thing, which I've been doing for almost twenty years. Good, honest work. For *Settright Road*, I worked on it in short bursts between 4 a.m. and 6 a.m. every day, just as I did for my second novel. If given a choice, however, I'd sit around and make shit up all day long.

READ ON

BONUS STORY: A MAN UNFIINISHED

First appearance in The Sun Magazine under the title "Green Street Incident"

I open my eyes and Carol Doda tells me to fuck off. Then it must be a couple hours later and I'm upstairs and it's dark and I'm thinking of quicker ways to kill myself. A far-off foghorn is warning ships away from the cliffs. It's a sad sound, long and low. I can taste on my teeth what I drank all night. Nancy Martini is asleep on her back on the mattress next to me. She's snoring and her store-bought tits rise and fall and her breath fills the room. It's not a bad smell; she smokes clove cigarettes, chews cinnamon-flavor gum. Her face is still pretty. The window that overlooks Green Street is open and there's a chill and I put the white sheet over her white legs; I want to protect her, keep her safe and warm. She moves a little and turns onto her side, facing away. I close my eyes.

Other drunks downstairs at Gino & Carlo's are playing pool and laughing. I can smell the pizza at Golden Boy's as well as the aftereffects of our eager but empty sex. I get out of bed, feel around the floor for my pants and shirt and put them on. Step into my shoes. I can make last call, if Frankie Junior is not too pissed at me. Nancy will be afraid if she wakes up alone, because she needs to refill her prescription, but that simply isn't something that I can worry about anymore. I need to find my own balance.

Frankie Junior sees me and shakes his head slowly but nonetheless gets down the dusty bottle of Old Crow. Pours a stiff one over dirty ice cubes. Sets it in front of me. He doesn't say a word and he doesn't have to and neither do I because his dad and me go way back. A fly lands on the lip of my glass. The Giants are on television and Barry Bonds pops one into McCovey Cove. I put the drink where it belongs and my throat warms. Tom Linehan rubs my shoulders like a cornerman at a professional bout. When I see my face in the mirror, I barely recognize it. Pete Crudo is belting out Sinatra tunes. He used to have a gig in Vegas. He keeps a condo in Boca and refers to Sammy Davis as "the muthafucka of muthafuckas." He sits next to me and buys me drinks until I'm thirsty again. He sees himself as a father figure. Then Tony Machi shows up with a flashlight and a plastic Safeway bag heavy with snails he found on the trail to Coit Tower. After keeping them in a cardboard box for a week, he'll roll them in cornmeal and brown them in sweet butter. He tells me the recipe twice—he says everything twice. This town is full of characters and I am the king of the misfits.

Then there's a problem near the bathroom and Frankie Senior wants me to take care of it because that's what I do. He'll give me a free refill. Some college kid punched a hole in the sheetrock after he scratched on the eight ball. He's built like a linebacker. I place a cocktail napkin over my glass and get up. The college boy tries to defend himself but it's no use since he hesitates and that is the worst mistake you can make against a guy like me. Nancy Martini says I have a mean streak a mile wide and maybe she's right about that. I take him into the alley and hit him until he stops moving but I don't feel mean about it. I don't feel anything.

There's a drizzle and the faded yellow curb is chipped and slick and I sit on it and roll a fat one to catch my breath. My lungs burn in that good way. A clean-cut young couple leaving the new bistro is looking sideways at the mess I have made. I smile and wave, blow smoke rings. It must be a scene. That wouldn't be a bad way to go— face-down in the street. But the kid isn't dead, he just needs some stitches and to give his ribs a rest. Fog rounds the corner like a gang of hooligan ghosts and a rat slips up from the sewer. I haven't had a meal in four days; Nancy cooks but I don't eat in hopes that I'll simply disappear. A skinny sapling with tiny red flowers pushes up from a crack in the sidewalk.

Frankie Junior mops the floor with poison while Frankie Senior counts the cash. It was a profitable night. He gives me a little for my trouble and also puts some aside to get the wall patched tomorrow. I finish my drink and say goodnight. Frankie Senior kisses my cheeks European style, bolts the door behind me.

My key sticks in the lock to the apartment as usual. Nancy Martini is squatting in a corner of the room, pulling her knees up against her chest. She woke up and got scared and now I feel like shit about it. I settle in next to her and put my arm around her and I tell her that everything is all right. I hold tight and rock back and forth. It's all right, baby, I say.

After a while she believes me and stops shivering and puts her head on my shoulder. Her heart flutters like butterfly wings. It's raining outside and coming sideways through the open window. I feel it on my face and neck and bleeding knuckles. Then she gets up and burns incense while I use my library card to chop up some gack on the glass-topped coffee table. She partakes and then does her version of a striptease. More for her than for me at this point; she needs to feel beautiful and desired. I clap my hands. She smiles, kneels naked in front of me, and puts her face in my lap. I stare at her flaking scalp, the dark roots of her bleached hair. She cries softly as she unzips me. Candles on the ledge, a siren in Chinatown. She puts me in her mouth. I close my eyes.

My brother the Queer rubs his eyes with his thumbs when mom tells us that he has a different father. It isn't so much the news as the cocaine he's just hoovered up his nose. My other brother, Jake, calls my mother a whore. He's the oldest, retired navy. We're sitting in the kitchen, wrapping up a family meeting. I'm drinking all the cooking sherry and everything else in sight. Earlier in the week, we learned that a bridge worker on the Golden Gate found Dad's wallet on the handrail and alerted the authorities. They checked the tides and the current and found him washed up on Baker Beach a couple days later. The saltwater had done a number on him. I hadn't seen the old man in years and don't recall what our rift was over; it was always something. Truth be told, I always figured him for a jumper.

It's a good thing Dad is dead, Jake says.

He's referring, of course, to my mother's news flash regarding her ancient act of infidelity.

He makes a sign of the cross, ends at his lips.

But on the other hand, this does explain a lot, he says.

I try to respond but it seems I no longer have the capacity for language.

Mom won't tell us who the Queer's father is. She says it's none of our goddamn business. I'm in no position to judge, especially since Nancy Martini gave me the boot again and I'm living in a broke-down RV in my mother's one-car garage—the same RV we used to take on road trips to Yosemite back when we were at least pretending to be normal. It's just a temporary arrangement. I don't expect to live much longer. Nancy Martini doesn't need me anymore because her goofball shrink can get her better drugs. I always knew it was just a matter of time, but that doesn't lessen the sting. She put all my things in a trash bag on the stoop with a note.

We've been through this routine before.

My mother is playing a Bing Crosby album that skips when Jake and the Queer start throwing hands over the estate—Dad wasn't rich by any definition, but there's property up north and a retirement fund. She tries to break them up with her metal cane and falls. Just like old times, I manage to say. She rolls over and gets stuck like a turtle under the card table. The boys keep slugging, ignoring her hopeless flailing. It is a sight. So fucking funny and pathetic and sad that I laugh. Eventually I help her up and then Jake puts the Queer through the kitchen window. Mom grabs her chest. Neighbors call the cops in Spanish. Officer Lopez radios an ambulance for the Queer's concussion and my mother's bad ticker. They ride together to SF General, where they'll stay twenty-four hours for observation. Alabama Street to Cesar Chavez to Portrero Avenue. Mission District cops are Latino tough and Jake gets pepper-sprayed and tasered and hogtied and he'll spend the night at 850 Bryant. He's a real fighter, that one. I'll pick him up in the morning, but it's nice to have the house to myself for a change. I try my mother's bed and it smells like the worst parts of her.

I smoke one of Nancy Martini's skinny cigarettes in the dark alley between Jesus Loves You and Adult Video. We're back together again, back on that fucking merry-go-round. It's past midnight. I hear what sounds like a cat dying about halfway down, where a fence has been erected, and I go closer to investigate. The poor stray took a busted chain link right through the eyeball. Maybe she got chased by a dog or a raccoon or maybe she'd been hunting a rat. She's stuck and really thrashing about, hissing at me like I put her there, looking at me with that one crazy angry eye spinning around in its socket. I let her get used to me for a minute and then I move behind and try to calm her with my voice. I put both hand around her ribs and count, one, two, three, and in one smooth motion slide her off clean, letting her go over my hip. Then the cat is gone so fast it's like she was never even there. A few scratches on my arm but not bad.

They say cats get nine lives and I wonder if that's a blessing or a curse.

Nancy Martini is comatose, which is normal for a Sunday. She danced Saturday at The Hungry I until two in the morning and then pulled a private party afterward. I know all about those private parties, but it's good money, especially considering her best years are far behind her. Last rainy season she told me that young girls with big tits were making the serious dough and she'd heard about a doctor in Redwood City; the Vietnamese woman who does her nails said he was the best and cheapest in Northern California. So I gave her all the money I'd just won on a fast horse at Bay Meadows. She had the procedure done the following month.

She's snoring now. I wash the cat off my hands and make a night-cap of Southern Comfort and warm milk and watch Nancy sleep from a metal folding chair. Her hair is wet, water staining the pillow, because she likes to shower after being groped by strangers all night long; I can't even imagine what that's like. There is an empty bottle of pills on the floor alongside a glass that is also empty except for a few melting ice cubes. She's wearing one of my old wife beaters and a pair of cotton shorts. I wonder what she's dreaming. I hope it's about having nice things. I hope I'm not in it. She's a good and decent girl and deserves more than I can ever give her.

When they stick my father in the ground, I'm wearing a monkey suit borrowed from my old friend Mike Shannon. There are nip bottles in the back of the limo and when empty they make music in my coat pocket. I'm riding with my mother and her friend Florence and my brothers. I close my eyes and wake up at Tony Nick's and the Giants have lost to the fucking Dodgers. A guy in an LA T-shirt says something smart to me and I put him on the floor and crouch over him and rain my fists on the parts he leaves unprotected. I'm not angry, there's no emotion, it's just a thing I do. The violence allows me to focus, to slow down the world so I can function in it. Everybody wants me to stop but there's no stopping me now. The jukebox is playing my favorite Johnny Cash song. Somebody grabs the old rotary phone to call for help. Fog from outside slips in the front door slow. A wood chair breaks and a door comes off its hinges and more fresh air wafts in off the bay. Broken glass. A flawless white tooth is lodged in the flat middle knuckle of my right hand. With my left, I have somebody by the ankle.

It takes four rookie cops to subdue me in the middle of Green Street while Sergeant O'Barry directs traffic around us and laughs and smokes a cheap cigar and tells them to cut off my circulation with the plastic straps they use now instead of metal handcuffs. He's been arresting me for years. I curse his mother and cat-hiss whiskey at him. He uses his boots on my face until one eye swells shut and then he eats a slice of pepperoni and mushroom from next door while his boys tuck in their crisp shirts and clean up with napkins—fast learners. O'Barry's chin is shiny with cheese drippings. They shove me in the back of his wagon and at North Station, use a hose on me that splotches my skin red. They give me a jumper that is too small and I stand freezing in a corner of the cell. Sergeant O'Barry sticks his head in and says, Sorry about your fucking pop.

I wake up in a soft bed and look at the sun outside. My eyes water so I pull the curtain closed. I don't remember being released, but my memory isn't what it used to be. There's a radio playing softly from the bathroom and somebody is banging a hammer in perfect rhythm next door. I get my bearings: I'm in Lorraine's studio on Market Street. She lets me crash here sometimes. Mornings she waits tables at a twelve-seat café on California and Polk. I look at the clock on the wall over the stove; her shift has already started. The small kitchen smells like oatmeal. There is a bowl on the counter and I get a spoon and scoop it all into the trash—the brown mush and the raisins and the walnuts. The thought of eating makes my stomach turn. I sit on a chair and smoke a cigarette and then another. Then I stand up and get sick in the sink. The hammer next door. I count my ribs in the shower and lead pipes complain and steam rises to the ceiling.

Lorraine shakes me awake by the shoulders. I open my eyes. She's wearing a big T-shirt that goes down to her knees. It's old and yellow and advertises Baby Watson cheesecake. I sit up and rub my face with my hands and she touches the top of my head. We stay like that for a while. The day is almost gone and I have the shakes. She smiles. Jesus Christ. Her smile always fills me with something new.

Boy, you gone to kill yourself.

Shit, girl.

Well, don't do it here.

All right.

I get up and she puts her arms around me and gives me a squeeze. I can smell the lotion she uses to keep her skin as smooth as polished wood. She's a beautiful girl. I let her hug me for a while and then she shakes her head and avoids my eyes. I find my clothes and get dressed and she goes about her business—putting some groceries in the refrigerator, hanging up the wet towel I left on the floor near the bathtub, checking her answering machine. There's a nasty message from a credit card company. She owes them a bit of money it seems. I owe her more than money, so when she's not looking I leave the remains of the cash Frankie Senior gave me next to the lamp on the end table. With any luck that will hold her over. I'm out of cigarettes too.

See you, I say.

You don't have to go.

Yeah, I do.

I can fix us a drink.

I shake my head. I'm tempted but I need to be out on the street for a while. That's part of my sickness too: uncomfortable indoors, near people, uncomfortable in my own skin.

I turn to the door and she follows me. I undo the deadbolt and open it, take a step so that I'm straddling the threshold. She puts a hand on my shoulder and I stop.

Call me later, she says.

All right.

I probably won't call her later. I won't even remember we had this conversation. But I don't say that. I hear the lock go into place and I dig my fists into my pockets. It's five flights down and the elevator is busted. The stairwell smells like piss. A crackhead is curled up at the bottom and I step over him. I open the door and the sky is bright and pigeons scatter into the street and shit on the pavement. A dented taxicab jumps the curb and almost runs me down and then rights itself and disappears. I don't even flinch.

Then John P. the bartender is complaining about washing dishes. It's Mario's on Grant and Green. It's mostly a bar, but they serve panini and salads and soft potatoes fried in recycled olive oil. I used to play ball with John when we were kids. He was a hell of an athlete. You wouldn't know it to look at him now. I can hardly remember what I was like back then.

It's just crap is what I'm saying, he says.

He keeps on about the dishes and I tune him out as best I can. John wants Mario to hire some Mexicans but the old man is too cheap. And besides, he thinks they'll rob him blind. He's racist against non-Italians. He hates some Italians too, but mostly he reserves it for the others. I nod my head as long as John keeps pouring. I drink until I feel normal again. There is some crap playing on the juke in the corner. I'm going to smash it to pieces. I close my eyes and try to get my mind straight. Then I'm sitting on a bench in Washington Square. A tall tree casts a long shadow on a faded brick wall. The smell of fresh-baked focaccia. Children running down the steps of St. Paul's. A line around the block for Mama's. Cars and graffiti-scrawled buses and messengers on beat-up bikes. And fumes.

Kevin Moretti stops his white pickup and taps the horn. He waves me over. He has work for me if I need some scratch. He runs a paint crew. We're going to a house in the Sunset District. It's an interior job. He'll give me twenty bucks an hour. We take Kearny to California to Presidio. There is fog and I get a chill and we double-park and get out for coffees at Tennessee Grill. It's mostly Asians in this part of town now. Then Kevin drops me off and gives me the keys and the house is empty except for buckets and brushes and heavy sheets to protect the hardwood floors and I paint the kitchen eggshell and the dining room a shade of purple and the hallway some sort of tan. The walls were already prepped, which is perfect. It's a good day's work. The backyard is overgrown with weeds and orange wildflowers that cling to a green vine. I sit on a stump and smoke a cigarette from the pack Kevin gave me as part of an advance. I hear the L train sliding down the hill on its copper-colored rails toward Ocean Beach, where whales go to die sometimes. The birds get to them and the dogs and the flies do too and the stink of it carries for miles.

Kevin comes back with a sixer of tall boys. He tells me about his golf game. He has a time share in Palm Springs. He did time at Lompoc and his neck displays the crude ink to prove it. We smoke cigarettes and drink beer and then we lock up the house and his

truck and walk to the Dragon Lounge. It used to be Fahey's. Kevin
runs a tab and we go into the shitter a couple times for a toot. Then
the place fills up with off-duty cops from Taraval Station and some
of them are all right with me and others are not. Kevin gets nervous.
The Giants are on television. Santiago hits a dinger. The girl behind
the bar is Chinese and is wearing a short skirt and a tank top and
silver dangling earrings. The cops are all over her and I don't blame
them for trying.

Nancy Martini won't come to the door. My old key doesn't work. I
don't know what I'm doing anymore. But there's a man in there with
her and she knows I will mess him up bad. She's going to ring the
police. I don't care about that. I call her a whore even though I know
it's not true, not the way I mean it. She begs me to leave and she's
crying. It seems she has forgotten how she used to need me and I say
as much. How soon we forget and all that nonsense. I just want to
talk—that's what I say and it was true at first but now I want to fuck
her also. Whoever is in there with her isn't making a peep so I probably know him from the neighborhood, or he knows me and what
I'm likely to do when I see him. Then my brother the Queer comes
to get me. Nancy called him at our mother's house. His eyes are big.
He's scared of me. Everybody is scared of me when I get like this.

Come on, he says. Let's go.

Fucking whore.

Come on.

He takes my arm and I let him because he's my brother and he
is soft.

You're lucky she didn't call the cops, he says.

I tell him he's the lucky one. He looks at me.

That I don't fuck you up, I say.

Oh, that. I thought you meant lucky I have you as a role model.

Yeah, that too, I say, trying not to smile.

But I laugh and he does too. The Queer can always make me laugh. Even when we were coming up. He tells me Jake is still pissed about the other night, mostly at our mother but also at him. I tell him not to worry about it. Jake will stay away for a few weeks, maybe go shoot some ducks at his camp near Russian River, and then he'll forgive and forget. The guy can't hold a grudge. It isn't in his chemistry. The Queer agrees and feels better now—except for the bruised skull Jake gave him Sunday. He's supposed to meet a guy at Kimo's. We take a cab to Pine Street and I pay for it. It's all pole smokers but I don't care. My brother orders a gay drink that is some kind of martini, which makes me laugh too. I buy a couple rounds for him and his buddy Nick, who seems like good people, and that puts me at ease; the Queer deserves to be happy. Then the trolley comes shoving down California lugging tourists to the financial district. I smell Greek pizza and Swan's oysters and the flower shop.

John P. tells me Mike Shannon is banging Nancy behind my back. I don't say anything. Apparently it's been going on for months and I'm the last to know. My head starts to hurt. I look around for somebody to hit but the joint is empty. He pours me a shot of Jack Daniel's. The front of his shirt is dry because Mario finally hired a Mexican. Then I soak the suit I borrowed from Mike in gasoline and burn it on the sidewalk. Mrs. DiMartini yells from her second-story sublet that she's going to call the fire marshal.

Lorraine invites me to dinner. She slow-cooked corned beef for her godson's baptism and has leftovers. Garlic mashed potatoes. Cherry-tomato salad with goat cheese. She puts it on a plate for me. I can't stand the thought of eating. I look at it for a few minutes and she sits there watching me. Then I tell her about Nancy Martini. At first she looks dejected, moves her chair closer to mine, takes my hands in hers and cries. My narrow wrists, blue-rope veins. She smiles. Jesus. There it is again. I almost smile too.

You're wasting away, she says. A fucking skeleton.

Right.

Well, now it's just you and me.

She's glad Nancy's out of the picture. She wants to mend me. She likes projects. Lorraine gets up and lets me take her pants off. Then I'm standing behind her and she puts me deep inside and we bump against each other like that for a while. That's how I fix things, make them right at least for the time being. Besides the various substances and the fights, that's the only way I know how. She wants me to finish but I can't and she gets upset and cries and so we keep trying until we're too tired. Finishing isn't critical to me—it's the trying. Once I'm there it's always disappointing; I end up empty and alone.

She falls asleep and I go into the bathroom until my hands are sticky with the mess I finally make. I clean up. The meal is still on the table. I stab a piece of cold meat with a thin layer of fat on the edge and take a bite. Chewing is unfamiliar and I go slow and I only gag a little. I use a stale heel of buttered sourdough to soak up the last of the gravy. Then the sun comes up over rooftops and among white clouds and a bony brown bird sits on a buzzing telephone wire. Startled, it flaps madly and disappears from sight but returns within seconds. There are others too, gray with yellow eyes and bigger wings, but this one stands out. I watch it forever. My head hurts and I get in bed and rest it against Lorraine. She whispers bullshit in my ear until I nearly believe it.

ACKNOWLEDGMENTS

These stories appeared, sometimes in different form, in the following publications: *The Stinging Fly* ("Just the Thing"), *Berkeley Fiction Review* ("Six Stones Down the Mountain," "The Mohawk Trail," and "Cut Me in Pieces and Hide"), *Necessary Fiction* ("Dark Days"), *SubTerrain Magazine* ("Storm Chaser"), *The Baltimore Review* ("Settright Road"), *Whiskey Island Review* ("Nice Sleep"), *Xavier Review* ("Barnyard"), *The MacGuffin* ("Nuts"), *Midway Journal* ("I Won't Wear Black"), *Dirty Dishes* ("Flunky"), *Front and Centre* ("Moon or Heaven"), *Event* ("Stay Where You Are"), *Wilderness Literary Review* ("Watch Out, Townie Boy"), *Puerto del Sol* ("Damn the Wind"), *Thought Magazine* ("Main Street Incident"), and *The Dalhousie Review* ("Listen to that Train Whistle Blow").

The author would like to acknowledge the talented and big-hearted people at Dzanc Books for agreeing to go on this journey with him and then never looking back. Damn the torpedoes.